Golden Eye
and the _____
Deadly Dancer

To Kaya

Frm. Santas
Anonymous
Merry X Mas.

Order this book online at www.trafford.com/08-0528
or email orders@trafford.com

Most Trafford titles are also available at major online book retailers.

Note for Librarians: A cataloguing record for this book is available from Library
and Archives Canada at www.collectionscanada.ca/amicus/index-e.html

Printed in Victoria, BC, Canada.

ISBN: 978-1-4251-7682-2

*We at Trafford believe that it is the responsibility of us all, as both individuals
and corporations, to make choices that are environmentally and socially sound.
You, in turn, are supporting this responsible conduct each time you purchase a
Trafford book, or make use of our publishing services. To find out how you are
helping, please visit www.trafford.com/responsiblepublishing.html*

*Our mission is to efficiently provide the world's finest, most comprehensive
book publishing service, enabling every author to experience success.
To find out how to publish your book, your way, and have it available
worldwide, visit us online at www.trafford.com/10510*

 **Trafford** PUBLISHING® www.trafford.com

North America & international
toll-free: 1 888 232 4444 (USA & Canada)
phone: 250 383 6864 ♦ fax: 250 383 6804 ♦ email: info@trafford.com

The United Kingdom & Europe
phone: +44 (0)1865 487 395 ♦ local rate: 0845 230 9601
facsimile: +44 (0)1865 481 507 ♦ email: info.uk@trafford.com

10 9 8 7 6 5 4 3 2 1

GOLDEN EYE
And The Deadly Dancer

Judith Anne Moody

Illustrated by
Rita Schoenberger

Dedication

In honour of the spirit of all First Nations People and the memory of my beloved husband, Don

Acknowledgements

The author is pleased to acknowledge the assistance of the following people: Karen Harry of Tsawout HQ, Laurette Ireland, Maryvonne Farrand, Rita Schoenberger, Robert and Ella Krull, Judy and Bruce Haley, Laural Grimes, Cory Ursulan of Cowichan Cultural Centre, Lillian Hunt and Andrea Sanborn of the Kwakiutl U'mista Cultural Centre, Guujaaw of the Haida, Barbara Joe of the Tsawassen First Nation (131), the staff of the Coquitlam City Centre, Red Deer and UBC libraries, Craig Miller, Julie, Colin, Ian and Terry Blow, Henry, Betty Anne and Dan Caldwell of Salt Spring Island, Anonda Berg, and John and Sybil Alexander who gave me life and love enough to believe in my stories, plus all my friends and family in B.C. and Alberta who loved and encouraged me.

Disclaimer

This book is primarily a work of fiction. Although I have endeavoured to depict the culture and legends accurately, I am aware that the very early First Nations told of "transformers" but that the actual practice cannot be authenticated. Also, the names have been simplified and are not according to the ancient ways. The Haida and Kwakiutl have given their blessing as have the Salish of Tsawassen (131) to use their legends but I claim no copyright on any First Nation legends.

List of Chapters

List of Illustrations

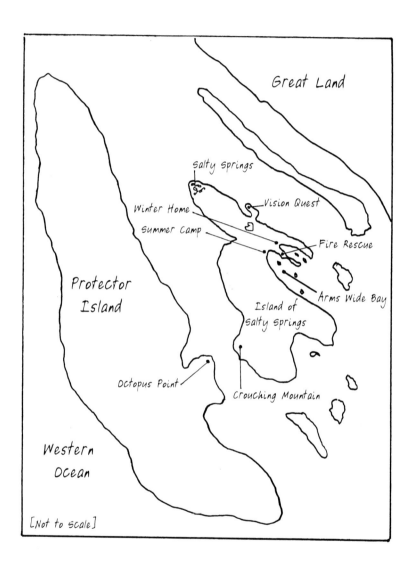

Great Land

Salty Springs

Winter Home

Vision Quest

Summer Camp

Fire Rescue

Protector
Island

Island of
Salty Springs

Arms Wide Bay

Octopus Point

Crouching Mountain

Western
Ocean

[Not to scale]

Chapter One

Magical Fire Rescue

Speckled sun danced on the forest floor and yellow leaves rustled beneath his feet as Golden Eye set out on his vision quest journey, many thousand years ago. The bronze-skinned, Coast Salish First Nation lad of eleven summers intended to follow the path around the bay and then up the eastern side of the Island of Salty Springs, his home. Crows and jays squawked above him, and a robin trilled her pretty song. The sun warmed Golden Eye's back. He felt good.

Crackle! What was that? He stopped and cast his eyes around. There, nearly invisible beneath an autumn-brown bush, lay a very young deer, its left front leg lying at an unnatural angle. The poor creature's eyes were wide with fear and pain, and its ears and nose twitched. It struggled, trying to rise and flee.

"Peace, be still little fawn. I am your human brother, Golden Eye. I see that your leg is broken. Feel my hand passing the great stillness into you. Now, with this piece of hide and these thongs I am binding your broken limb. My people will care for you until you can go back into the forest with your own kind. I am going on my vision quest but I think you have been sent to be my first challenge," he said softly, smiling. "Peace, little sister, all will be well."

With a crash, Fat Goose entered the clearing and yanked at his big brother's arm.

"Come on, there's a fire!" yelled the boy. "It's heading straight for the summer camp. Father wants you to help load up the canoes and get the families out of there. Hurry!"

"Be quiet, Fat Goose," commanded Golden Eye. "Lay your hand on this unfortunate deer while I climb up and check the safest direction to go."

As quick as a raccoon, Golden Eye scrambled up a tall pine tree, and just as quickly came right back down.

"It's too late, Fat Goose. The fire is coming right for us. We're cut off from the village except by water."

"What are we going to do, brother? I'm scared. I can't swim, and what about this little deer?" Fat Goose's face crumpled as he began to cry.

"We must be brave, little brother. Now, pick up our injured friend - gently, gently. Bring her down here, by the water."

Golden Eye knelt by the shore and began to enlarge an otter den in the bank with a piece of driftwood. His heart beat rapidly as he struggled to control his own fear.

"I'll make this den a little bigger so you can both hide in there. Climb in there now - carefully, keep her leg still," he said, helping them into place. "Now, lie there quietly until I come back with my canoe."

Golden Eye turned and walked into the green-blue ocean as smoke began to curl around his shoulders. He struck the surface with his flat palm and called out "Eeeeyeeeee, yeaw, yeaw, yeaw." As he swam out, his orca friend, Black Fin, surfaced beside him. Golden Eye wrapped his arm around the killer whale's shining black dorsal fin and was carried across the bay to the village in a moment.

"Thank you, Black Fin," Golden Eye called back to his friend, "now you dive back to safety."

Grey Fox listened to his son's words of danger and pointed to Golden Eye's canoe resting on the gravel beach. Grey Fox was tall and strongly built, but lines of worry creased his face. There was so little time to get everything and everyone into the big canoes and away from the onrushing fire. Even as they spoke, bright flames crackled and leapt into the crowns of the nearest trees. Together father and son lifted the small canoe into the water.

"Go quickly boy. Get your brother and meet us out there in the wide channel."

Golden Eye paddled with strong, hard strokes toward the otter den. Twenty strokes out he hesitated. Smoke was so thick on the water now that he couldn't see the spot for which he was headed. Golden Eye closed his eyes and listened to the spirits within him. Then, with his inner eye, he clearly saw the otter den. He opened his eyes and struck off in that direction.

After a dozen strokes, the smoke cleared before him. Golden Eye rose onto his knees, his shoulders stiffening. There in the water, between him and his goal, stood Crooked Paw, a huge old black bear. The water was the only safe place for him too, but he was angry! He was angry that his paws were singed and that smoke burned his eyes and nose. He wanted someone on whom to vent his anger. Roaring furiously, Crooked Paw swung his great paw with its deadly claws at the trembling occupants of the otter den. Fat Goose cried out in terror!

Golden Eye tilted his head as if he heard something over the roar of the fire. A faint blue aura appeared around him. Golden Eye had joined with the Spirit of the Air and became invisible to the giant bear. Silently he paddled to the otter den. Fat Goose passed him the tiny doe with smoke-blackened hands. His face was soot black too, and streaked with tears. He whimpered as he scrambled into the canoe.

Crooked Paw sniffed the air but stood completely still.

The canoe slid silently away from the shore, blending with the water and smoke. Dip, swish, dip, swish. Golden Eye propelled them all smoothly away from danger, away from the bear and the fire, toward the big canoes and their family.

The boys met up with the family canoes as they paddled away from the fire, out of the big bay where they summered. Occasionally, someone would look back at where camp had been, watching tongues of flames lick out over the beach where they had eaten and worked and played together.

"Earth Mother's fiery broom clearing out the old and making way for the new," intoned Uncle Raven Claw from his paddling place in Grey Fox's canoe.

As they paddled around the point and down the long harbour toward their winter home, the people watched in terror as the fire advanced toward their longhouse. Golden Eye stared at the only home he had known. Something stirred inside him - a rage, a need to do something. Quickly he beached his canoe on one of the two islets in the harbour. He raced to the top and stretched out his arms, leaning into the hot wind that blew from the roaring fire. Then Golden Eye roared. He roared back at the fire, his face contorted, the veins in his neck distended.

Astoundingly, the wind veered sharply. The fire turned back upon itself and slowly went out.

The canoes landed and everyone piled out. The bigger and stronger people lifted the others onto shore and unloaded their hastily stowed belongings and caches of winter food. In a few hours they were settled in, safe and sound, with just the memory of the fire burning in their memories. Golden Eye was patted and hugged and thanked. Some people just shook their heads in awe; some laughed for joy.

Little brother Fat Goose, his eyes filled with wonder, craned his neck to look into Golden Eye's face.

"How do you do these things, brother? Where

does your magic come from?"

"A gift of the spirits, perhaps. I don't really know." But as they settled into bed that night they both wondered how it had all begun.

Chapter Two

The Special One Arrives

West Wind surfed in over the rolling Western Ocean waves, slid up and over the mountains of Protector Island and swirled into the village of the Salish, the People of the Salmon, who dwelt on the Island of Salty Springs. West Wind twirled the peeling, rust-coloured bark and thick leaves of the arbutus trees and tickled the feathers of the raven, high in an ancient cedar. The people were gathered for their evening meal around a crackling fire. The men had spent the day catching and smoking salmon, the women and children gathering berries for it was eighth moon and time to prepare for winter.

A short distance from the village, Whispering Dawn and her husband Grey Fox stayed alone in their cedar-thatched alder pole hut, awaiting the arrival of their firstborn. They had fasted and frequently bathed to purify themselves for the special moment.

West Wind blew a gust of air into their haven, and a strong birth cry was heard. Old grandmother Robin Song entered to clean and wrap the infant; then placed him in his father's arms. Grey Fox stepped out of the birth hut and the people gathered near him. The child opened his eyes, drawing gasps from the people. They saw that the baby had one brown eye like all of theirs - but the other was golden - like a wolf's!

"A very special child you have fathered, Grey

Fox," exclaimed their shaman, Strong Oak, who was Grey Fox's father and grandfather to the newborn. "A returned spirit, I think. We must have a great potlatch for the naming of our great chief's first son. What will you call him?"

"Golden Eye. He must be called Golden Eye!"

replied Grey Fox.

Grey Fox raised the child above his head and prayed, "Great Spirit, make me a worthy father for this special one you have sent us."

"Wah! He is cursed! He should be killed before he brings disaster upon all of us!" exclaimed Screaming Jay, the spirit dancer.

"We will wait and see, my brother," said Grey Fox. "Perhaps it is blessings he will bring." High above them on a rock bluff, the one-eyed leader of the wolf pack raised his head as the moon rose and howled. Then, all through the forest, his brothers took up the thrilling chorus.

Twelve moons had passed since the birth of the Special One.

The day began simply, like most days of late summer for the People of the Salmon. Yawns and stirrings were heard; then people began to come out of their shelters to greet the day and each other. Some took time to stand still in the gentle coolness of dawn. They breathed in the pungent scent of the bright green pines and cedars as the morning breeze swished through their branches. Long, sinuous limbs of arbutus trees stretched over the sea bank, their twisted trunks glowed russet where the bark peeled itself back. Their thick leaves shivered, shining in the soft early sunlight.

The sky at dawn was a soft blue with only puffs of white clouds. Thought prayers of thanks were sent to the Great Spirit for another fine day. Children went off into the bush to relieve their bladders, calling out to one another, already making plans for their games. Everyone bathed in the ocean and then rinsed off the salt in the little waterfall of the stream.

Soon the women busied themselves with cleaning and dressing the little ones while the men stirred up the coals of the communal fire. New flames leapt up as they added more wood. The women and older girls prepared the morning meal of boiled salmon and bowls of blueberries. This they washed down with fresh, cold water that young boys and girls had brought from the creek in tanned animal bladders. The families gathered around the fire and sat on stout cedar logs. Talk and laughter increased during the morning meal.

"Another good day for fishing, Red Squirrel," offered old Limping Goose.

"Yes, I saw many shiny-sides biting at flies on the surface when I went down to make water," said Red Squirrel, who was tall and heavy-set at twenty-seven summers. "We'll catch many cod today out by the rocks, then we should take the canoes around by the narrows to see if the chum salmon are running yet."

Black Cod, small and slim at nineteen summers, chimed in, "I saw deer and bear tracks up by that nice quiet pool where the creek drops over the big rock. I think I'll tighten up my bow, take a few good arrows and bring us back big meat for winter. You fellows had better save lots of energy for the carrying and carving. You know I'm the best hunter in the village."

"Big talk from a little man," laughed Grinning Badger, grown heavy at forty summers. "You'd better take some of the little boys with you so you can rest your bow against their backs. You look pretty scrawny today."

Black Cod whooped and pushed Grinning Badger off his log seat. He held him down in a playful wrestling match. All the other villagers chuckled at the sight. The children jumped up from their mothers' sides and ran to watch, chattering excitedly.

"Hey you two!" grumbled old grandmother Robin Song. "You're getting dirt in the bowls. Get up and get busy or I'll have to beat you with my walking stick. I know you remember how the knobs feel on your backs from when you were bad little boys."

The two men helped each other up, chuckling at the memory of those so-called beatings – mere taps on their shoulders she had given them – but a definite reminder to behave.

With that the group began to separate. The small children snatched a few more blueberries and ran off to play behind the alder pole and cedar mat shelters that were their summer homes. The women and girls cleaned their boiling bags, hung up the water skins inside the shelters to keep cool and began to air and clean the shelters after the night's sleep – ready for the next one. Then they took their children and their bowls and baskets in search of berries.

Whispering Dawn carried Golden Eye part of the way to their family's berry patch and let him toddle along the rest of the way. Everything interested him. He stopped to investigate rocks, rain puddles, scurrying rabbits, birds fluttering in the underbrush and fish jumping in the beaver pond.

The men and older boys divided into groups for cod or salmon fishing, bear and deer hunting. Each knew of the special strengths or weaknesses of the others, and they went off to hunt or fish, each according to his skills. Much food would be needed to feed the ten families of the village during the winter ahead. It was good work for men - good to fill their days with useful action for their strong muscles.

Screaming Jay, supposedly on an expedition to collect feathers for his dance cape, struck off into the woods, with murder in his heart.

Two of the older men, Brown Wolf and Many Stars, stayed behind, one to carve alder eating bowls, and one to make new arrow and harpoon heads. A few of the older women too, stayed near the warmth of the fire, weaving new carrying bags and baskets out of strips of split cedar bark and spruce roots.

"How do you make those coloured strips,

Grandmother?" asked Spotted Fawn.

"Yellow comes from tree moss or the roots of oregon grapes. You get black by burying them in mud or steeping in hemlock bark infusion. Now red is harder. To make red, someone has to make pee-pee in an alder bowl. Purple comes from huckleberries," Robin Song said over the sound of Spotted Fawn and Young Birch running off, giggling about peeing in a bowl.

"There is never an end to making new baskets is there?" sighed Crooked Maple. "They finally wear out, just like our old joints."

"Pity someone couldn't weave us some new joints," groaned one of the old ones.

"The years give a time of strength and vigour, and then they take it away, warning that our treasure of days upon the earth is nearly spent," replied another.

The women grumbled softly to each other while they tried to outdo one another with their beautiful patterning and their weaving that was so tight it was waterproof. Their baskets were so fine that they were very valuable for trading throughout the islands and up and down the coast of the Great Land.

Screaming Jay circled back to where Whispering Dawn harvested ripe huckleberries. He waited silently, crouched down, chanting inwardly, his eyes glittering with hatred for Golden Eye. As he chanted, his form began to waver and change. He

turned himself into a big, green toad, just the thing to interest Golden Eye and draw him into the water to drown while his mother's back was turned!

Back at the camp, Shiny Water called to her daughter of five summers, Young Birch.

"Come over here, daughter. Let's set up the loom under that big arbutus so we can listen to the water spirits talking while we weave you a new skirt," she said, her long, fine braid falling over one shoulder. "Bring me my baskets of soft bark strips and some dog hair, will you?"

"Oh, good!" exclaimed Young Birch. "I love it

when you weave that white dog fur around the top so it's soft against my skin. Can I bring Spotted Fawn too, to watch?"

"That would be all right," said Shiny Water. "She's a good girl, but her mother doesn't weave as fine as we do. She should learn the right way," she said, somewhat vainly.

In a while, the men brought home their fish and game, which they cleaned and hung or spread over the fires. The women were still picking berries.

Suddenly a piercing scream shattered the

stillness of the day! Grey Fox recognized his wife's voice and lead the group running to find her. She knelt on the mossy bank of the beaver pond. Golden Eye, dripping wet, was cradled in her arms.

"What's wrong?" yelled Grey Fox, along with a chorus of concern from the villagers.

"I found our son lying face down in the water," moaned Whispering Dawn. "He was right beside me one moment, and the next moment, there he was, out on the pond, just floating, not moving. I thought he was dead!"

"Is he all right now; is he breathing?" asked Grey Fox, grabbing Golden Eye up, checking him all over.

"Hop, hop," said Golden Eye (a clue that no one noticed).

"Yes, he seems to be fine," Whispering Dawn replied. "I don't think he got any water inside him – he didn't even cough or spit out any water!"

"Thank the Great Spirit," sighed Grey Fox.

The rest of the villagers expressed their gladness and thanks and returned to their chores. Whispering Dawn caught at her husband's arm to hold him back.

"Grey Fox, I must tell you something, although I do not know what to think of this myself. I – I'm sure I saw your brother, Screaming Jay, slip into the trees beside this pond, not ten steps from where Golden Eye lay in the water. Can this be so? Surely he would have gone to save the boy, not run into the forest?"

Grey Fox stiffened. He looked from his son to his wife, then to the pond and the stand of birch beside it. His heart was heavy.

"I don't know what to think either," he said "but remember what Screaming Jay said when our son was born last summer, that he was cursed and should be put to death? This makes me wonder just how it was that Golden Eye came to be in among the wolf pack last moon."

"Well, our boy is obviously blessed and not cursed because the wolves seemed to love Golden Eye, especially their leader, the one with only one eye. You saw how they rubbed against him so gently. Do you think Screaming Jay could have had something to do with that too?"

"I'm not sure, but he was certainly very close to that scene too. I saw him paddling away in his canoe in the bay, just down the bank from the boy and the wolves."

"But why – why would he want our son dead?" asked Whispering Dawn in anguish.

"I don't know!" exclaimed Grey Fox. "True, his son Green Duck would inherit my Great Chief status, my crests and songs, my belongings and my fishing and harvest rights if Golden Eye wasn't around, but Screaming Jay has plenty to leave his son on his own. As our head spirit dancer he has much prestige and

many good fishing spots and berry patches to leave to Green Duck. Shouldn't that be enough?"

"It would be enough for the many who have less, but perhaps not for Screaming Jay. Green Duck is much too gentle to be a great chief anyway – not like our little ball of fun and energy, right Golden Eye?"

Golden Eye smiled at her over his father's shoulder and gabbled in the secret language of the very young.

"One good thing," said Grey Fox softly to his wife, "soon this little fellow will be old enough to talk and tell us everything that happens. Screaming Jay will not dare to attack him near home then."

The couple walked slowly back to the village with a strange cold worry in their hearts. They vowed to be ever vigilant to save their Special One for his true destiny.

Chapter Three

First Magic

On a fine spring morning, old Grandmother Robin Song took Golden Eye, now of three summers, out of the great longhouse to play near her while she worked. He no longer needed his diapers of coiled, soft-shredded cedar bark, and his head-board, previously strapped to his forehead to create the back-sloped shape of the highborn, had been removed.

Just outside the door stood the man-sized, man-shaped greeting post with its right arm raised.

"*Kla-how-eya, tillicum.* Hello, friend," Golden Eye waved and called to it.

Beyond them stretched a long, wide, very gradually sloping gravel beach leading down to the head of a long inlet of the ocean. A small lake - a pond really - shimmered off to the right of the longhouse, and a creek dribbled down from it to the ocean. Golden Eye loved to wriggle through the tall bullrushes while

Grandmother Robin Song dug up some root bulbs of the rushes for dinner with her sharp-pointed stick.

"You can't see me, Grandmother. I'm invisible," he teased.

"No, I can't see anything but your black hair and your brown face," said Robin Song. "You're invisible all right."

"Oh, Grandmother, look at the blue butterflies," he called, his voice full of wonder.

Grandmother Robin Song looked up and saw the three blue butterflies fluttering delicately about. Up and down and around and around in circles they cavorted, like mad puppets. Yet, when Golden Eye stretched his hand out to them, the butterflies froze in flight, two feet in front of his eyes.

Grandmother stood speechless, watching as Golden Eye studied the elegant creatures before him. After a few moments, he brought his hand down to his side and turned to face Grandmother Robin Song. The butterflies resumed their aerial dance.

"Aren't they wonderful, Grandmother?" cried Golden Eye. "I wish I could fly like them. Why are we stuck on the ground while all the birds and butterflies can just rise up and fly wherever they want?"

When the astonished old woman regained her voice, she sat Golden Eye down on a log and spoke.

"Each earthly creature to its own place Golden Eye. The Great Spirit gave us the earth and the heavens, the ocean and all the creatures of the water and the land and the sky. He put each being and creature in its proper place so that we may all live and breathe and eat and share in the goodness of the world. Only our spirits can fly away from the earth."

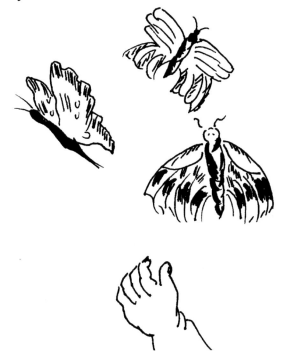

"My spirit can fly, Grandmother? How do I make mine fly? I'd like to look down and count the trees and see where the rabbits and foxes are hiding. When can I do it, Grandmother?" pleaded Golden Eye.

"Be patient, Grandson," she replied. "Strong Oak is our shaman, our spirit leader. He will instruct you in these matters. It is true that you are marked as a chosen one of the spirits. You have looked into the still surface of the lake and seen your lovely golden eye. You are the only human with this special eye. The way you made those butterflies hold still is more proof that you are special. I have never seen that happen before, and I have lived many, many summers."

"Where is my spirit, Grandmother?" he asked in wonder.

"Deep within you, little one," she said. "Within your heart and your mind, your eyes and your hands. It is what makes you more than a bag of bones with a dirty face."

"Ha, ha, ha," laughed Golden Eye. "I'm a bag of bones."

He felt himself: arms, legs, chest, and face. Sure enough, there were bones inside his bag of skin and this so amused Golden Eye that he took Grandmother Robin Song's hands and danced around and around until she was out of breath and begged to stop. They sat upon a driftwood log.

"I'm going to throw my spirit up there to sit on top of that little grey cloud. Watch me," Golden Eye yelled happily. He flung up his arms and stretched his face and body forward. Then he became very still, his body relaxed, his voice quiet for several long minutes. Grandmother Robin Song was filled with fear, yet she kept very still. She could see that Golden Eye's spirit had left him and she was afraid that it might get lost in

the heavens, maybe even devoured by the Soul-Eater
Spirits, if she startled him before it returned. She began
to rock gently and croon in a soft voice, calling gently
to his spirit to return to the boy. She did not touch him.
Then, with a sharp intake of breath and a stiffening-up
of his body, Golden Eye became lively again.

"Well, Grandmother," exclaimed Golden Eye,
"that was fun. Everything looks different from up there
- sort of squashed down. I saw the top of our longhouse
and my wolf friend with just one eye over there in the
forest watching us, and I saw a lady's face in the clouds

but I couldn't hear what she was saying. I did see lots of trout in a bunch over there by that tangle of fallen trees in the lake. We should go get our fishing spears and catch some of them for dinner, don't you think?"

Tears of relief and happiness sprang to old Robin Song's eyes and she agreed. Yes, they should go fishing now. She would have done anything to keep his unschooled spirit safe within his little body. She determined to speak to Strong Oak this very day and tell him he must begin the boy's spiritual training at once!

"Also, Grandmother," whispered Golden Eye in a conspiratorial way, "I saw how many grey hairs there are on top of your head, but I won't tell anyone!"

Robin Song picked up her grandson in her still-strong arms and gave him a very big hug.

"Those grey hairs are the totem of my years, little one. Each one bears witness to the times of hunger or accidents or when loved ones died. I still miss my birth family although it is so many summers since I was captured from them," said Robin Song wistfully.

"What does that word mean, Grandmother, captured?" asked Golden Eye, wriggling to get down.

"That means I was born in a village far away, up Protector Island. One morning, while I was asleep with my family, many men rushed into our longhouse. They struck down our men and tied up some of the big boys and younger women.

The last thing I remember of my home village is the sound of my mother weeping. We were taken away in their long canoes and became slaves in their village. I was pretty lucky though. After a number of summers, I slipped away from the berry pickers, stole a canoe, and paddled for days. Your grandfather found me, half-dead, and soon after, we married. And so I came to your village and I have been happy here.

Those boys they took weren't so lucky. They had to work very hard and were not given much food. Some were beaten. They were made to sleep right by the door of the longhouse so that they would be the first to be injured in case of a raid. Some of them died. One of them, my brother, Duck Wing, swam away one day. I don't know if he got somewhere safe. I hope so.

Anyway, Boy-With-Many-Questions-In-His-Mouth, in this way we have come to be together and for this I thank the Great Spirit. Right now I want to dig some water lily roots for dinner too, so will you hold this basket open please?" asked Grandmother Robin Song.

Golden Eye was silent, absorbing all that his Grandmother had just told him.

"I am sorry you have had sad times, Grandmother," said Golden Eye in a soft and thoughtful voice. "I'm going to get big and strong soon, and I'm going to wake up early every day and watch so no one comes to take any of us away. I wouldn't like that."

"Hmm," muttered Grandmother. "It's good I have you to take care of me alright, but we will see what the spirits have in store for you, little man."

When Robin Song had enough of the tasty roots for the evening meal, she lifted the basket and hung the straps over her shoulder. Holding his hand, she walked back to the longhouse with Golden Eye. She left him there watching a group of older boys playing a game with a ball made of woven rushes and went inside. There she found Golden Eye's father, Chief Grey Fox, the shaman Strong Oak, and the rest of the individual family chiefs sitting in council. She quietly joined them and listened as they decided village matters. Then she reached for the talking stick. When it was passed to her she spoke.

"Young Golden Eye this morning sent his spirit out of his body," she said.

"What? How did he know to do that? Did you tell him of this old woman?" Strong Oak demanded angrily. "He is too young; he has not learned about fasting and contacting the spirits in the trance and how to ensure that his spirit does not lose its way and be taken by the Soul Eaters while it is out there! There is great danger for the uninitiated in this. Where is he now?"

Robin Song related the events of the morning. She explained how she had chanted to call his spirit back to his body. She told them what Golden Eye said he had seen from above.

"Then it is true," spoke Grey Fox, thoughtfully. "We are thankful that you were with the boy and sang his spirit back, my wife's mother. I think it is time that you begin his instruction into spirit matters, Strong Oak," he said. "Otherwise, who knows? He might show his trick to all the other little ones and pretty soon there won't be a young spirit left in the village. They'll all be off floating in the sky," said Grey Fox with a grin, trying to lighten the atmosphere.

Strong Oak agreed and promised to give some time each day to Golden Eye.

"It seems there's no doubt that he has a strong spirit force but it must be carefully developed to use it safely. It's not going to be easy though, with a boy of only three summers. He has much to learn before he goes on his vision quest to seek his own guiding spirit."

"That won't happen until his eleventh or twelfth summer. Try to remember when you were that young, Strong Oak," intoned Grey Fox with a sly smile, "if you can remember that far back. All the rest of the elders must share in his training too, by answering his questions and sharing the history and the stories of our people with him. Beyond that, we must let him run and grow."

"I still say he is cursed," muttered Screaming Jay. "You'll all be sorry you didn't listen to me."

An uncomfortable silence prevailed as the leaders rose and left the longhouse. Golden Eye, unaware of their various concerns, ran and played among the other children.

Chapter Four

The Legend of Crouching Mountain

"Come on, Tan Buck, I'll race you to the top of Crouching Mountain," called Golden Eye to his best friend. They set a burning pace for boys of eleven summers. Golden Eye, taller and slimmer, ran lightly and lithely. Tan Buck, more sturdily built, ran with powerful strides. After the first sprint they settled into a comfortable rhythm for the long run, along a path beaten smooth by centuries of running feet.

Just inside the green canopy of the forest, the one-eyed wolf kept pace - his tongue lolling out of the side of his mouth - staying near Golden Eye as he did nearly every day.

Before the sun had risen one hand's breadth higher in its daily path they had reached the base of Crouching Mountain and began the long climb. They ran deftly between the tall trees and through the dense undergrowth until the incline became too steep, and here they slowed to a fast walk.

At this point the old wolf turned back. It seemed he just enjoyed the run and the silent communion with the boys but felt no need to climb mountains with them.

The boys grabbed onto overhanging branches to pull themselves over big fallen logs and out-cropped boulders of granite. The incline at the peak was very steep indeed, almost straight up. Their breathing became ragged as hand over hand, rock-by-rock, and branch-by-branch they struggled upward, loosened dirt squirting away beneath their bare feet.

Finally they reached the zenith of Crouching Mountain, and for a minute or two they sat down, panting. A bald eagle swooped near, decided they were too large to carry home, and soared away.

"This is great," panted Tan Buck with a laugh, "I can look an eagle right in the eye!"

When their breathing normalized, the boys stood in their secret stance, back to back, arms wide, turning slowly, step by step in a complete circle at the very top of the mountain. The wind swirled in their fine black hair as they chanted their secret chant:

> "Spirits of the earth
> and spirits of the seas,
> Come into our bones
> and make us strong as these"

Golden Eye and Tan Buck observed their world spread out around them. Dozens of islands large and small filled the brilliant blue ocean in all directions on this bright, sunny day. The whole world seemed fresh and clean, the air tangy, after the last few days of rain.

To the West they saw the massive Protector Island, crenellated with inlets and headlands, studded with evergreen forests and lush valleys, and crowned with its own range of mountains. Its northern end could barely be seen. To the North and South were many smaller islands of different sizes and shapes, as if the Great Spirit had sprinkled precious gems upon the salty sea.

The boys gazed East toward the Great Land. There was no end to it North or South and it continued to the eastern horizon. Great ranges of sharp-tipped mountains ran row after row down its length, some still bearing the snows of winter on their brows.

"There's my favorite mountain on the Great Land," declared Tan Buck, "that one that's taller than all the others with snow all over it. It reminds me of my mother wrapped in one of her goat-fur blankets. I want to climb it some day."

"It's my favorite too, especially when the sun or the moon rises behind it. Sometimes a plume of steam comes out of the north face there."

"No kidding! My father said his grandfather's grandfather's grandfather saw it erupt when it was an active volcano. The earth shook all the way over here. Flames shot up high and the smoke of a thousand fires rose above it. Then a river of what they called lava - burning liquid rocks - ran down the side of the mountain! It must have been awesome!"

"Awesome alright, but look at our island. I think it's the most beautiful of all the islands! It's shaped like a huge spirit dancer don't you think? See the three sections? The top one looks like a ferocious dance mask. Arrowhead Lake over there is its eye and that long peninsula and inlet are its nose and mouth. See our longhouse at the head of the inlet? It narrows there like a neck where we camp for the summer. This middle section is like a big pair of shoulders with folded arms, tapering beneath them like a man's waist. The third section looks like a belly with that beautiful flat valley. The other two mountains are his knees drawn up. I'm always glad when we can do this run and climb again."

"Why do we call this Crouching Mountain?" asked Tan Buck.

"Aha," crowed Golden Eye, "that's a great story. You see over there, those boiling waters in the narrows between our island and Protector Island? Long ago, at that place we call Octopus Point, deep in the waters lived a monstrous, evil serpent named Shuh-Shu-Cum, Old Open Mouth. He lay in the water at the point with the tip of his snout out of the water. If any men tried to pass through the rapids, Shuh-Shu-Cum would suck in all of the water; all the canoes and the travelers in them. The travelers were never seen again. Now this caused great concern to all the elders of our many Salish villages. Our chief's son offered to try to kill Shuh-Shu-Cum. He was not afraid, he claimed, but the chief said the people had lost too many brave sons already. Runners were sent out in all the four directions to seek a solution. One brave had another idea. He had heard of a giant, Sum-ul-quatz, with the strength of a thousand men who lived near Tsawassen on the Great Land.

This brave lad borrowed a canoe and paddled his way in and out among the islands and then straight East for half a day to Tsawassen where he met Sum-ul-quatz. He told Sum-ul-quatz of the great sadness in the Salish villages because of so many deaths caused by Shuh-Shu-Cum, the hungry one. He hung his head then in sorrow and exhaustion. Sum-ul-quatz, the giant, took pity on him and offered to slay Shuh-Shu-Cum. Sum-ul-quatz walked down to the shore and there found a number of boulders, each the size of four large men.

One by one he lifted them to his shoulder and heaved them toward Octopus Point. One by one they fell in the wrong spots because this mountain was right in the way and too tall and jagged. Sum-ul-quatz and our brave ancestor then began to pray. They begged

this mountain to squat down enough to allow the boulders to pass over it. Their prayers were so fervent and humble that the spirit of the mountain heard them and drew down its top. The very next boulder sailed easily over this mountain and landed with a mighty splash right on top of Shuh-Shu-Cum, crushing and killing him.

Now, even though the narrows run fast and deep, our people are safe to travel there thanks to the giant Sum-ul-quatz, our clever ancestor, and the Crouching Mountain."

"That's a fine legend, Golden Eye," said Tan Buck in a tone of hushed admiration.

"I heard that tale from Eagle Claw when he visited from our ancestral home on Protector Island. He is a great storyteller. I hope he will share more of our legends with me. I want to be a great storyteller too, when I grow old. And you will be the greatest spirit dancer ever born when your training is finished," he said grandly. "When will the ceremony take place to send your spirit into the clouds for your final testing? Are you afraid? I have heard it is a very frightening time."

"It will probably be about the same time as your vision quest, the ninth full moon of our eleventh summer and yes, I have some fear. I'd better get rid of it though because I have been told that no fearful soul can make it through the time with the dance spirits. What about your preparations for vision quest; are you learning lots from the old shaman? When do you think you'll be ready for your vision quest?"

"By the end of this month, just like you, I think. That's pretty scary too, going away alone and trying to contact the spirit world. I can't wait to meet my protecting spirit though. We can do anything if we put our whole self into it, my father says."

"Right, of course we can, as long as the Soul Eaters don't get us."

"Okay, come on. Let's gather some of these garlic mushrooms for our mothers and get going home."

"All right, but let's go down the other side of Crouching Mountain for a change. I know it's really steep but hey, we're the two strongest, bravest young Salish lads alive aren't we?" bragged Golden Eye.

"No doubt about it," agreed Tan Buck. "On to adventure!"

Chapter Five

The Cave of Gold and Danger

After carefully packing the small, delicate, very pungent mushrooms in their shoulder bags, the two intrepid friends began their descent. Old rockslides had left long bare patches of sheer granite and treacherous piles of loose rock. Hardy, projecting tree roots gave them purchase though, and they finally reached the dense scrub brush below the slides.

Tan Buck set his foot on a good-sized rock to traverse to a clearer area. That rock, and a hundred others beneath it, gave way. Tan Buck frantically reached for something to grab onto in order to save himself from the shear drop of fifty feet. There was nothing there! Just as he began his plunge, Golden Eye's hand grasped Tan Buck's extended forearm and swung him over to a sturdy bush. Golden Eye had wrapped his legs over a stout branch and hung down to reach his friend.

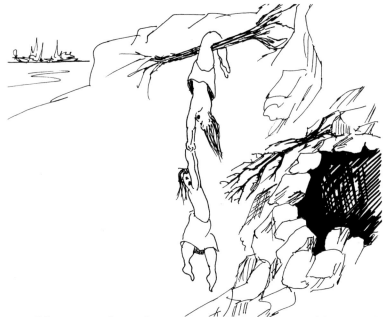

No more than three seconds had passed but both boys clung to their perches, sweating and panting, speechless with the understanding of what could have happened. Tan Buck turned his head to where the rocks had been.

"Hey, there's a cave here!" he exclaimed, stretching his foot over to it, while still hanging tightly onto a thick branch. "Let's go in and rest for a minute."

"I'm all for that," replied Golden Eye. "I feel like a possum hanging here."

The cave was so dark that the boys couldn't see more than twenty feet into it, but it was the smell that really got to them. How many years or centuries ago had the rockslide covered up the mouth of the cave?

"Yuk, it smells like old rotten salmon eggs in here," gagged Tan Buck.

"Or a hundred moldy baskets of putrid berries," whispered Golden Eye, holding his hand over his nose and mouth. "Here, bruise this cedar frond and hold it in front of your nose to kill the smell. Let's take a look around."

Once their eyes adjusted a little to the darkness, the two friends began to investigate the cave. It seemed to penetrate far back into the depths of the mountain.

"This is so amazing!" exclaimed Golden Eye. "Hey! Why don't we go back to the mouth and grab a nice pitchy pine branch to make a torch and look further? I've got my flint rocks to light them."

"Good idea," replied Tan Buck.

Off they went and soon had torches blazing. Fifty feet into the cave their torches began reflecting off the sparkling stalactites and stalagmites and something even brighter on the walls. The bright patches became bigger as they walked quietly, deeper and deeper into the cave. The boys stopped to investigate.

"This must be gold," said Golden Eye. "I have seen some of this as a decoration on some beautiful carvings our fathers brought back from trading journeys. It is very, very valuable because it shines without rusting and can be hammered into many shapes. We should take some of this back home. Just think how treasured our potlatch gifts will be with some of this on them, and how important our families will be when they own it."

"I'm glad we brought our knives to dig it out," said Tan Buck. "Hey! What was that sound, like someone groaning?"

"I didn't hear anything. Come on, let's get some more gold. Then we have to get going. I'm supposed to study with Strong Oak this afternoon," replied Golden Eye, while prying out a large nugget.

The next moment the cave was filled with a strange, green mist and a sound, growing in intensity. It began like a whispered voice, and grew louder and louder until it was a mind-piercing shriek. The mist grew denser and seemed to form the image of a man, but such a man! His face was deeply grooved and his mouth open in the shape of one howling in great rage. Wild, misty hair flew about his head, intertwined with what seemed to be seaweed or stringy moss. The image of a ragged blanket encircled the spectre's shoulders and arms. Those arms and the gnarled, horrid hands at the end of them, stretched toward the boys.

Golden Eye and Tan Buck screamed and covered their ears, trying to shut out the awful howling noise, but to no avail; the sound seemed to pierce their very bodies. They could hardly move or breathe. Both boys had dropped their torches to cover their ears, and the torches went out.

"Tan Buck, we have to do something to defeat this thing," Golden Eye screamed at his friend. "Here, take these pine branches. Pretend they are wings and do your best Thunderbird dance. I'll drum on this hollow log and chant. Come on, we have to fight or it will kill us!"

The boys forced themselves upright and launched into their strongest, loudest possible defense against the ghastly, evil presence that surrounded them. On and on they chanted and danced, buoying each other up and encouraging each other in their desperate quest. One hour went by, then another, as the two best friends pitted themselves against the horrible, howling spirit, focusing their minds and spirits on the image of triumph.

With a sudden inspiration, Golden Eye reached into his pack and withdrew the very pungent garlic mushrooms. He set them down in front of himself. Amazingly, the spirit seemed to shrink. Golden Eye set out the mushrooms from Tan Buck's pack as well, and the howling lessened audibly. The boys took heart and renewed their onslaught against the evil one. Then, as Tan Buck began to flag, his legs buckling, and Golden Eye's voice became hoarse, the rays of the late day sun pierced the gloom of the cave and; with a final grim howl, the spirit vanished. Golden Eye and Tan Buck collapsed onto the floor of the cave, exhausted and panting.

"Thank the Great Spirit that's over!" gasped Tan Buck.

"Exactly," replied Golden Eye, weakly. "Now, what do you say we get out of here before the sun sets and that THING might come back!"

"I'm right behind you, if I can even crawl. What on earth was that thing?"

"Probably nothing on earth. Maybe the spirit of some ancient, evil shaman that got trapped in here to judge by his power."

"Or a spirit dancer, they have a lot of power too."

Goose flesh rippled over Golden Eye's body. He didn't know why, but some deeply buried memory was stirred.

"At least it's downhill from here. Come on, pick up those wonderful mushrooms and I'll grab some of this gold. I swear I will never complain about the smell of those mushrooms again. Let's go home!"

Two hours later, two very tired and hungry boys dragged themselves into the longhouse with an amazing story to tell!

Days later, Golden Eye returned to chisel into a flat, granite boulder a warning to any who might approach the cave.

Chapter Six

Lessons with the Shaman

"The most important thing to learn is to listen. Go to a place where you can't hear the noise of people and listen. Come back in five days and tell me what you have learned," intoned old grey-haired Strong Oak. His shoulders were stooped and his muscles stringy. His face was lined with a tracery of wrinkles and tanned from many summers in the sun - his grey hair forming a striking contrast. He had a slight limp from an old injury and as he moved toward the entrance of his shelter, he tripped and lost his balance. As he fell, he assumed the form of a bird - an owl - and spread his wings to rise before hitting the ground. In another second, he returned to his human form. Golden Eye sat open-mouthed.

"I'm sorry about that. I must be getting very old. I used to be able to control when I transformed, but lately it just happens whenever my failing body needs a little help. Now go."

Golden Eye returned after five days.

"I heard many things, grandfather. I heard squirrels running, climbing and chattering. I heard bears snuffling and munching berries, ducks paddling in the bay and calling to their little ones. I think I even heard an ant crawling up a blade of grass."

"Not enough; listen deeper, listen with your skin and your eyes and your hair."

Once again Golden Eye took time each day to be alone, apart and to listen.

"I heard more," he told Strong Oak, who had been curled up on his sleeping robe in the form of a furry raccoon! He awoke and returned to his human form.

"I heard the change in the sound of the wind before sunset and before the rain comes. I heard the difference in the sound of trees, each one telling me of subtle changes coming in the weather and the season. I heard the animals move at different speeds when they were hunting or running to hide or making a nest for napping.

The birds too told me many things: their chattering when things are going well, their screams when predators are near. But their silence - that tells me even more. When birds are quiet, something is very wrong. I also heard the sound of my own insides: my heart beating and my stomach churning, which was funny. Is that what you meant by listening, grandfather?"

"You have done well. But there is more to hear. Our people exist in the area between the undersea world and the forest, with the great dome of the spirit world above us. Before our time, spirits, ghosts, humans and animals, all lived in the great darkness. When raven brought us light, people began to be brave and take their place. The ghosts shrank into the dark places, and the animals found their homes in the sea and on the land. The spirits could take the shape of anything they needed or wanted to, to help or to fool people or to marry a beautiful human.

All these things too you can hear from within yourself - the world of the spirits. You will then understand the power and responsibility of the special gifts you have been granted, your connection with the spirit world <u>and</u> the earth. By really listening to it you will open your mind to full knowledge and power.

We will speak often. Bring me your questions and we will share both worlds with each other. You must be aware of the spirit world and able to reach it and enter it before you go on your spirit quest to learn of your own protecting and guiding spirit. You will rely on it to assist you through difficulties in your life. And while you are listening, your own spirit song will come to you.

Most importantly, the spirits must get to know you and make you welcome so that you will return from their world at the end of your vision quest."

"Thank you grandfather. I will keep listening until I hear the spirits talk to me. Now I must go; my mother wants me to take care of my little brother and sister for a while so she can get some weaving done."

Chapter Seven

Brother, Sister, Magic

"Did Grandfather Strong Oak really turn into a bird and a raccoon?" quizzed Fat Goose.

Golden Eye had chosen to take Fat Goose and Silent Dawn for a picnic in a sunny glade not far from the longhouse. He had built a small fire and, after praying to their spirits and offering a small gift so that they might give themselves to him, was roasting a pair of squirrels he had caught for their lunch.

"Yes," chuckled Golden Eye. "I often have to wait for him to wake up to continue his lessons. But you know what? His nose always twitches just before he wakes up – that's how I know he's waking up."

"What other animals does he turn into?" Fat Goose asked, fascinated. He had never seen anyone turn into anything, and he wondered if Golden Eye was telling the truth or just another of his famous big made-up stories.

"One time he fell asleep after drinking some tea with honey in it. He must have been thinking about how bears love honey because he turned into a small black bear, right there on his sleeping mat."

Fat Goose pondered this silently. He was six summers old now, a sturdy, stocky little fellow, born five summers after Golden Eye. Fat Goose picked out a little tune on the flute that his uncle had brought back from a trading trip to the Great Land. He tried to imitate bird songs and the nearby birds, quiet at first to hear this strange new sound, began to answer as he got better at mimicking their songs.

Silent Dawn was only two summers old. She had never said one word, and everyone knew she never would. Although she was beautiful, with soft, full lips and eyes like big, liquid, brown pools, her birth had taken too long and the Soul Eaters of the spirit world had carried off her mind. She was blessed with very good health though and was loved, welcomed and cared for by everyone in the village. Everyone but Screaming Jay who said she was cursed by her brother's golden eye. Silent Dawn happily played with a stick this day, drawing lines in the dirt.

"You have spirit powers," said Fat Goose to Golden Eye. "Can you turn into anything else?"

"I don't know yet," came the reply. "Strong Oak says that maybe, if the need is strong enough, someday I might be able to. I'm supposed to join my spirit with his."

"How? How can you do that? Isn't your spirit inside you? How can it reach someone else's?"

"Ohhhh, stop chattering for a while, will you? I don't <u>know</u> how! Here, help me with the lunch. Pass me the squirrels and I'll cut them up. Then put some more wood on the fire. It's getting too low."

Fat Goose did as he was asked then turned to watch Golden Eye dividing up the meat.

Behind them little Silent Dawn, imitating Fat Goose, rose to throw her stick in the fire too but she lost her balance and fell face first toward the fire.

Golden Eye felt an alarm inside his head! He dropped the food and whirled toward the fire, then flung out his right hand. Fat Goose spun around to see why. There in the midst of the fire lay Silent Dawn! She did not cry or move. Her little stick was still within her fingertips but the fire and even the wood within it were frozen - frozen solid. Golden Eye reached her side in one step and snatched her up into his arms. He cried. He cried great sobs of relief because she was alive. She was not even burned. She would, however, for the rest of her life, carry a flame-shaped dark image up her whole left arm. Silent Dawn smiled up into Golden Eye's face as he kneeled down to let Fat Goose hug her too.

"You sure are special, Golden Eye," said Fat Goose reverently. "I bet even old Strong Oak couldn't have saved her like that."

Golden Eye gathered his chubby, talkative little brother and his silent, smiling baby sister in a warm hug and sighed a huge sigh. Lunch tasted extra good after that.

Chapter Eight

Freedom Wings!

"Stretch up as far as you can, boy. Okay, I've made a mark there. Now, step back and look. That's how long your canoe will be."

Raven Tail was the master canoe carver of the village and he had agreed to create Golden Eye's first canoe.

"Great! This is great, Uncle Raven Tail!" exclaimed Golden Eye. "My own canoe! But you're not going to cut this whole great big red cedar tree down for one little canoe for me, are you?"

"No," smiled Raven Tail. "We'll just ask this fine tree for enough of himself for the canoe, place a little gift of thanks beneath him, and then let him go on growing for another hundred summers. Only for the big, many-person canoes do we take down a whole cedar. You see that dip on the other side? That is where my grandfather was given enough for my father's first canoe."

"Why do you use red cedar and not some other kind of tree?"

"The Great Spirit gave us many kinds of trees but more importantly, he gave us the sense to find the best purposes for each one."

All the while he spoke, Raven Tail's eyes darted along the wood and his hands felt their way along and around the tree, getting to know it with his finely tuned senses.

"Yellow cedar, we have found, has very dense, fine-grained fibres, best for carving totems and masks, things like that. Our women make baskets and our clothes from the inner bark. See those places where the outer bark is gone? First those women ask the tree's spirit for permission, then they make a notch down low on the trunk, grab a bit of the softer, inner bark and pull up quickly to get a nice, long strip to work with.

Those maples over there, their wood makes beautiful spoons. Our shaman makes his rattles out of it too. See this spot where my grandfather pushed a stone into the bark of this old maple? It has grown out around the stone into this big lump. Here, I will cut off a square and you can carve something out of it."

"What can I carve, uncle?"

"Just start carving. The wood will tell you what is hidden within it."

Uncle Raven Tail continued notching, wedging

and hammering at the would-be canoe as he continued talking about the trees that he loved. He loved trees as others loved winning at sporting games or as parents loved their children - not just to share his knowledge but also to share his love and his wonder at these gifts of the Great Spirit

"Now this alder here, it has no taste so we use it for eating and serving bowls. Fir, hemlock and spruce we use for building and for firewood and fine spruce roots for our fishnets. But when we find a good old yew tree, ah, that's the hardest of hard wood. We can use it for clubs, hammers, wedges; anything that needs to be really hard. It's practically like rock."

"Red cedar though," he said lovingly, smiling and stroking the rough, deeply creased bark, "red cedar is like a great, gift-giving father. It is so easy to split to make the great long planks of our longhouses. All our canoes are made of it because it doesn't rot and without canoes how would we travel to all the other villages with news or to trade? How would we get to the fishing grounds? Its branches, leaves, and its bark too, all have uses: for medicine, for clothing, for brooms, for our bent boxes, for roofing our summer shelters. Yes, we thank the Great Spirit for red cedar, and for our brains and hands to make use of it."

Golden Eye watched as his uncle marked out the length, width and depth of his canoe and then worked with his stone-headed axe and yew wedges to remove

Golden Eye and the Deadly Dancer

that section of the tree. All the while, Raven Tail hummed and chanted, thanking the great cedar for the gift of part of itself for the boy's canoe. All the while too, Golden Eye carved away at the lump of maple until it became a seal on a rock.

When the section of tree was ready to come away from the tree, Golden Eye's father, along with Red Squirrel and Black Cod, came to help lower it and carry it to the ocean shore. They carried it out into the water and let it float. Raven Tail studied the wood, watching how it floated. His focus was very intense. He made a few marks on the wood while it floated, and then they carried it ashore. Golden Eye gave his carved seal to his mother. She was pleased.

"Never, ever drag your canoe over the rocks, Golden Eye," cautioned Raven Tail. "You must show respect and care for your canoe so that it serves you for many summers."

"How long will it take, Uncle Raven Tail, until it's ready?"

"It will take as long as it takes. First we let it dry out then I mark out the part I need to remove. I must listen to the wood and let it tell me things through my fingers. I will use my bone chisels and my adzes to take out some of the centre and then I will light small fires to burn out a lot of the centre wood. Don't worry; I won't let it burn right through! Fire is a friend as long as it is under control, remember that."

56

Day after day, between his chores, his running and his games, Golden Eye watched as his uncle coaxed a canoe out of the slab of wood with his chisels and hatchets and his many different adzes with their blades of nephrite, shell and horn.

"Can't I do something, uncle? If it's going to be mine, shouldn't I do some of the work?"

"Look in that bag over there. Get some of that sharkskin and I'll let you help sand the rough spots. Don't overdo it though. It's all balanced. Tomorrow we're going to fill it with water and hot rocks and when the wood relaxes, we'll put in the crossbeams to widen the centre and to add seats. Pretty soon, my anxious one, you will have your canoe."

"Thank you, Uncle Raven Tail. Have I said thank you enough times? I can already feel myself gliding across the water in my canoe. I'll be free from the shore, free from land. I'll be able to go anywhere I want, whenever I want!" Golden Eye ran in a circle with his arms out like wings.

"Not without a paddle you won't. Let's go find some nice hard maple and make a couple of boy-sized paddles. Remember that. Always carry a spare paddle. Your hands won't get you home very fast. We also need some good hard fir for the rim. Cedar wears down too easily; it's pretty soft. We'd better make a bailer while we're at it too, in case some of the ocean decides to take a ride in your canoe."

Finally the day came when the canoe was ready and so it was launched: Golden Eye's freedom wings! Between dawn and sunset, every moment he wasn't doing his share of the village work and his lessons with Strong Oak, the boy was paddling. He paddled around their bay, down the long reach of the inlet, and around the small islets with their colonies of gulls and cormorants, seals, mink and otters.

At first he had to wrap his hands in strips of softened cedar bark to prevent blisters, but soon he had grown his own set of paddling calluses and began to race his older cousins around the entire island.

Sometimes he would go alone for the sheer joy of being solitary with the sea and sky, feeling as free as the eagles soaring above him.

Other times he and Tan Buck would paddle away together, exploring all the bays and inlets of the Island of Salty Springs, all the driftwood-laced beaches, the towering cliffs, the hidden, mossy streams and the gushing rivers.

"You know, I think we could spend every single day from now to forever exploring all these islands and never finish," whispered Tan Buck one golden day as they rested in the shade of overhanging ferns. They were watching a great blue heron standing silently, one-legged in a shallow bay.

"You're absolutely right, my friend," Golden Eye whispered back, "but I intend to paddle far beyond our islands some day. I want to travel to the Great Land and meet all the people of the other big villages, maybe even go on a great trade journey with Uncle Green Willow, someday maybe."

"Yes, Oh Great Traveler and future Mighty Shaman," Tan Buck joked, "but for now, let's go to the island of the white dogs. We need to see if there are still plenty of rabbits for them to hunt and comb out some of that lovely soft fur of theirs. Our mothers are making white fur blankets as fast as they can for potlatch gifts and you know they never stop reminding us to go and get them some more."

"Don't I know it, and maybe tomorrow we should see if some of our older cousins would like to go with us to the Big Land and collect some mountain goat fur too. I hear it just sticks to the bushes when they shed their winter coats. A few bags of that should keep our mothers busy for a while and we can try to find some flint rocks up on the mountains too. But you're right; let's go see the dogs. There might be some new pups to play with too."

Paddles dipping in easy rhythm, the lads swung the canoe around and headed for White Dog Island. The heron roused himself from his silent, one-legged fish vigil and beat his great wings, rising vertically. Then he swooped before the bow of their craft, sending a dark, rippling shadow across the boys.

Golden Eye shivered. He didn't know why but a premonition of trouble crossed his mind. Just for a moment he thought he saw the face of a young woman in the water. She seemed to be trying to tell him something. Then the vision faded in the green and shiny depths.

Chapter Nine

White Dogs, Killer Whales and Near Death

"Get off me, get off! You're drowning me with spit, you silly dogs!" yelled Tan Buck.

Golden Eye sat nearby, his lap full of fat, white puppies, laughing helplessly at the sight of Tan Buck play-wrestling with three young males of the crowd of small, ecstatic, white dogs.

"Stand up, why don't you?" he called to his friend.

Tan Buck struggled to his feet, wiping his face on the dogs' woolly sides. He held out his hand, palm down, and the dogs lay down, quietly watching his face to see if he might want to play some more. Although the boys had run with them and play-wrestled with them for an hour or more, the dogs still seemed ready to keep on playing.

"That's enough play time, boys," Tan Buck told the dogs.

"Here you go, mommas, here are your babies back." Golden Eye nestled the wriggling pups against their mothers' milk-filled bellies.

"Where did I leave my good bone comb?" Tan Buck asked Golden Eye. "I think the bone combs are better than the maple ones don't you? They don't seem to catch in the fur so much."

"It's right here beside me on this rock, Mr. Forgetful. We'd better get the fur and get going soon. It seems the rabbits have had lots of babies too, so no need to worry about enough food for the dogs. The fresh-water spring is still leaving a nice, full pond of sweet water too, so it looks like everything's all right here.

I brought the dentalia rake along and I want to stop on the way home and try to scoop up some of them. Father says he needs lots of those lovely spiral shells for his next trading trip and for potlatch gifts too."

"My big sister sews them on her dancing dress. I like the sound they make, jingling against each other."

"White Daisies likes deer hooves better for that, and they're easier to get than dentalia. Too bad the dentalia only live that deep in the ocean – as deep as three men standing on each other's shoulders. I can dive pretty deep, but not that deep. All my breath gets squeezed out of me."

"Ooooh, White Daisies, your little girlfriend! When are you going to marry her?" teased Tan Buck. He had noticed how Golden Eye got red-faced whenever White Daisies smiled at him.

"Keep flapping your tongue like that and I'll have to tie a knot in it," Golden Eye stormed.

"Never mind, the rake works pretty well at scooping up the shells. Let's go get 'em. Goodbye boys!" yelled Tan Buck.

To a chorus of joyful barking, Golden Eye and Tan Buck pushed off and paddled away. Tan Buck leaned his head back and howled and the white dogs, one after another, tipped their heads back and howled too. Far off, their brothers of ancient time, the wolves of the forest, answered. The two lads laughed at the wild chorus they had started and headed for the dentalia bed.

FOOOSH.

Tan Buck and Golden Eye jumped at the sudden sound. They swiveled around on their seats and saw, not ten feet from their gunwale, a small male killer whale, no more than twelve feet long, its eighteen-inch black dorsal fin perfectly erect. Its small eyes were looking right at Golden Eye and its mouth was slightly open, revealing many, many teeth. It didn't move. The boys didn't move. Finally, after what seemed like many seconds, the young orca wriggled forward and touched the side of the canoe with his nose, gently,

obviously meaning no harm. Golden Eye looked right into the eyes of the beautiful beast. He smelled its fishy breath and he felt his spirit connect with that of the little whale.

"Welcome, my brother Black Fin," he said softly. "Do you want me to join you in the water?"

The orca wriggled back a few feet. Golden Eye had his answer. He threw off his garment and was over the rail and sliding smoothly into the chilly, green water in less than a heartbeat.

"Stay in the canoe, Tan Buck," he called back as soon as his head cleared the surface. "Follow us, but not too close, all right?"

Tan Buck, awestruck, just nodded and moved to the front of the canoe. He grabbed his paddle and tried to keep up.

Unnoticed by the boys, someone else was watching the event. Among the few trees on tiny nearby Bird Island, Screaming Jay, solitary as usual, slipped down to the shore and climbed stealthily into his canoe.

Golden Eye swam beside the young whale, diving and spinning, trying to keep up with his new friend. While under the water, the whale sang to Golden Eye a beautiful, haunting, pleading song, full of trills and clicks and musical squeals. Golden Eye tried to sing back.

With a good lungful of air he dove and tried to imitate the song in his throat.

The orca dove toward the fairly shallow bottom and Golden Eye followed, as far as he could, seeing all the wonderful creatures down there. Boy and whale surfaced at once. The orca, breaching and flipping, landed on its side with a huge splash. Then he swam gently up beside Golden Eye, sliding underneath his arm, right up to his dorsal fin. Golden Eye understood. He grasped the shining black fin, took a huge breath and down they went.

In one smooth, swift dive, they streaked toward the bottom. This way and that, through kelp beds and over shining white banks of sand spangled with purple starfish and scuttling crabs they sped, spying strange clusters of tube-like plants and wondrous rock formations as they careened through the underwater wonderland. Schools of fish scattered before them.

Golden Eye very slowly let streams of air bubbles escape but, of course, he ran out of breath first. Up he zoomed to the surface and gulped in great lungfuls of precious air. Right behind him his new friend broke the surface and kept on going, twenty feet into the air, then arched and slid back into the water with hardly a ripple. Golden Eye laughed with joy. He knew he could never do that.

Tan Buck and the canoe were but a large speck on the water.

Suddenly, from behind a great rock jutting out from Bird Island, a canoe appeared. Golden Eye saw the movement from the corner of his eye. He turned

toward it, just in time to see a seal harpoon streaking toward him. Golden Eye leaned to the left and the harpoon whistled by his head, so close it carried away some of his hair. He felt just a sting from the blade on his scalp. Before he could fully recover, however, another spear was on its way.

Golden Eye's spirit called out to that of his grandfather, Strong Oak. What should he do? Without even asking the question, the answer came. Change into a seal - and he did. The seal that was Golden Eye dove with a power and speed the boy could not have mustered. The second spear had been thrown too hastily and he watched it arc into the sandy bottom. He swam underwater as far and as fast as he could, twisting, diving and swerving, but finally, his lungs screaming, he had to surface.

His head swiveled, searching for his enemy. Golden Eye saw someone, black-cloaked, his back to the sun and in a swift canoe, paddling with all his might toward him. Quickly the man shipped his paddle and brought up a bow. He notched an arrow with lightning speed and sent it zinging toward the seal that was Golden Eye. Golden Eye twisted and dove but the shaft of the first arrow lodged in his left flipper arm, the razor sharp flinthead protruding. The second arrow he managed to avoid but the third was dead on target for his spine when a paddle intervened! Tan Buck had arrived.

The next arrow was notched and aimed directly at Tan Buck who sat defenseless in the small canoe. Suddenly, astoundingly, just as the arrow was about to fly, the man's canoe rose up out of the water and was flung onto the huge rocks of the island, propelled by twelve feet of angry orca. The man flew even further up onto the tree-covered island. His cloak fell from him. Was it – could it be – Uncle Screaming Jay? Whoever it was scrambled away over the crest of the islet.

Golden Eye returned to his own shape, and he and the orca swam toward each other. They were silent and still for a few moments when they met. Then Golden Eye reached out and stroked his friend's black and white forehead.

"Thank you, little wolf-of-the-sea." He whispered his thanks over and over as he shivered, realizing how close he had come to the end of his life.

Hooking his good arm around the orca's dorsal fin, Golden Eye urged him toward Tan Buck in the canoe. The special beast understood and propelled Golden Eye there.

Very tired and solemn, Golden Eye hauled himself into the canoe, stroked the whale's forehead again and watched it submerge and head off toward its pod which was gathered, waiting for the young one, a few hundred feet away.

"What just happened?" Tan Buck asked in a

shocked tone while he tended to Golden Eye's wounded arm. He used his obsidian-blade knife to cut off the head of the arrow and then quickly but smoothly withdrew the shaft by the tail end.

"I think I just nearly had my last great adventure," replied Golden Eye, rinsing the blood off his arm. " Let's go home. I need to talk to my father."

Chapter Ten

Good Medicine, Bad Medicine

Golden Eye awoke. He lay still and looked around his home. His eyes lingered on the broad, horizontal cedar planks of the walls rising to the back-sloped roof. They took in the massive cedar logs supporting it that formed the greater boundaries of the longhouse. Long food-drying racks hung above his head. The family areas were separated by low plank walls and hanging blankets. Each one's cook-fire was at the far right front of their area so that the smoke rose and exited through the central roof vents.

Sleeping platforms lined the walls and under them, bent boxes decorated with wonderful carvings of killer whales, salmon, otters and ravens held their belongings. Golden Eye's family, as befitted the great chief's family, occupied the space at the head of the longhouse. There was comfort in the sameness of all the old things. His father's words from the night before still rang in his head.

"I am sorry it had come to this, my son. There is no doubt that this is one of Screaming Jay's arrows. He alone feathers the tip like that. Now I must tell you that Screaming Jay has been suspected of attempts on your life since you were very small."

"What kind of attempts?" Golden Eye asked in amazement.

"During your second summer we found you lying face down in the lake. We thought you were drowned, and my brother was seen not far away."

"But I followed a giant toad into the water, and the lady I saw in the water told me not to breathe."

"Screaming Jay knows how to transform himself into other creatures. We think he lead you into the wat— what lady in the water?"

"Sometimes in dreams or times like you just said I see the face of a lady, someone not of our village. She seems to want to tell me things but I don't always hear her voice. I hope I meet her some day."

"I think you will," Grey Fox intoned, astounded once more at his special son.

"Another time, when you had barely begun to walk, we found you in the midst of the wolf pack and I saw Screaming Jay paddling away in the bay. Again he was foiled and it was a wonderful thing to see. Not only did the wolves not kill you, they all moved around you, brushing against you and whining softly while you leaned against the old black, one-eyed leader and petted the rest of them. We were amazed. I didn't want to believe such evil of my own brother, but after this last attack, I think there is no doubt. I will have to talk to the other family leaders. I'm sure he will be banished at the potlatch. In the meantime, you must avoid contact with Screaming Jay. He hasn't come back yet anyway, has he?"

"Why would he want me dead?" Gooseflesh spread up Golden Eye's back as long-buried memories began to surface.

"With you out of the way, his son Green Duck would become leader of the village and inherit all his lands, crests, stories and songs and mine too. It is terrible what greed can do to a man if it is his nature. You sleep now and leave this to the elders. We'll take care of it."

Sleep had been a long time coming, but in the cool light of dawn some of the clouds of fear dissipated from Golden Eye's mind.

"Come with me," called Grandmother Robin Song. "I'm going into the forest to get some fresh alder bark for that wound on your arm. I need a few other things too. With the potlatch coming up, I'll need plenty of medicine on hand. I'm teaching White Daisies my remedies, but you should learn some too, since you'll be going on your vision quest soon."

"I'm coming, Grandmother. Just let me dive in

the bay for a minute. I need to wake up and the salt water makes my arm feel better too."

"All right," she called, "we'll wait for you."

The morning mist swirled low among the tree trunks, floating over the moss. Fingers of sunlight began to pierce and dissipate it as the trio entered the ancient forest. A raven called raucously from high in the treetops. Old One-Eye the wolf caught their scent and came to investigate, settling onto a mossy bed just out of sight. Grandmother Robin Song notched and pulled off a strip of alder bark and bound it to Golden Eye's wound.

White Daisies, now twelve summers old, with ruddy cheeks and wisps of hair escaping her braids, watched intently, learning the medicine woman's craft.

"Please dig me up some blackberry roots," Robin Song asked Golden Eye. "They're very good for colds in the winter time. Here White Daisies, fill this little basket with those oregon grape berries - they make a good poultice. Get some roots too; I make a tea out of them for upset stomachs - everyone eats too much at potlatch. I'm going to take some of this cedar gum too; it's helpful for toothache. Let's see. Oh! I'll need some buttercup leaves for headaches too."

"What about this plant, grandmother?" asked White Daisies about a tall, purple-flowered weed growing in the gravel at the edge of the forest. Out of respect for her age, all the children called Robin Song grandmother.

"That's stinkweed. Rub a leaf and you'll find out why. That one needs much respect. Our spirit leaders use the leaves, very sparingly mind you, to induce dream-filled trances. You may be instructed to take some along on your vision quest, Golden Eye, but be very, very careful with it. Too much can cause insanity and a horrible, agonizing death!

"I'm never touching it, grandmother, never,

never, never," vowed White Daisies, her eyes wide with fear. "It sounds worse than those bright red mushrooms with the white stems and white dots on top. So beautiful, but I know - one bite and I'm one dead girl, right?"

"Right, and you are much too young and smart and pretty to join our ancestors on the burial island, so pay attention and remember what I tell you."

White Daisies ran ahead of them toward the village. Golden Eye and Old Robin Song rested on a fallen log.

"I am troubled, grandmother," said Golden Eye in a low voice, his head bent and tears near the surface. "I have pain that is much deeper than the arrow wound in my arm. I am in sorrow that my own uncle would want to kill me. I have loved him all my life, but suddenly I must watch over my shoulder whenever he is near. I feel so bad that I am the cause of trouble between my father and his brother too. I love my brother Fat Goose so much that I can't imagine ever mistrusting him or having to send him away. Help me, grandmother, I don't know what to do!"

"You have always been one to trust all those you love and every other creature on the earth," replied Old Robin Song softly, taking the boy's smooth hand in her old, gnarled one. "It doesn't occur to you that evil lives in some people and in some creatures too! This is a very hard lesson you are learning, but a valuable one.

The cost of safety is watchfulness. Give up a little trust - gain balance. This is a new sense you are adding to yourself and it is good. It may save you, and all around you, from danger in the future. Count it as another blessing from the Great Spirit; a giant step forward in your growing up. Come on now; let's get home. There is still lots to do to get ready for potlatch."

Golden Eye helped his old grandmother up, noticing how small and frail she had become but still so full of wisdom and kindness. His heart swelled with love for her as he walked slowly home beside her. He knew that his life would not have been nearly as rich without her.

Beyond the fringe of fragrant cedar boughs, Old One-Eye seemed to melt into the forest.

Chapter Eleven

Good Clean Dirty Fun

"Shhh, look over there," whispered Tan Buck as he peered through the tall sedge grass.

"What am I looking for?" asked Golden Eye. "Oh, yes! The otters have made a mudslide. Let's see if they will let us slide too."

Golden Eye, Tan Buck and six other young people were on a mission to collect clams on a bright, sunny morning the day before potlatch. They had hours of work ahead of them, but no one could pass up this opportunity for some good clean, dirty fun. It had rained for several hours the night before, and a newly formed stream drained the hill above the clam beach.

Golden Eye led the way, crawling on his belly, waiting until the otter pair went down the slide; then he slid down after them. The mud felt cool and wet and squishy on his belly as he slid out onto the sandy beach. The otters jumped in surprise to see him, sniffed him as he lay still, accepted his right to be there; then scampered up the hill for another slide. Golden Eye was right behind them.

The rest of the clam-digging expedition joined in the game one at a time, some quitting as others started so the otters weren't overwhelmed with young humans. After a while though, the mud began to dry up as the sun warmed the hilltop and the otters dashed across the beach and swam away. As a group, the gloriously filthy kids washed themselves off and got to work. They filled baskets and carrying bags with clams that gave away their location by squirting water in tiny fountains from within their sandy domain.

"Look at that funny long rock there, at the top of the hill," said Young Beaver, a boy of seven summers. "I wonder how it got there?"

"My mother told me that long ago, the tribes from the north liked to sneak up on our people here to kill and to take slaves," murmured Spotted Fawn, a girl of thirteen summers. "Our men learned to prepare for them. They kept a supply of loose boulders up there that they would shove down on the raiders as soon as our clam diggers were out of the way. One woman, my grandmother's grandmother, Squirrel Woman, had the sharpest eyes in the village so she was always posted as a lookout. Then, when she got too old, she lay on that hilltop and asked the Great Spirit to turn her into that rock so that she could always watch over us."

"Wow, I didn't know that," exclaimed Young Beaver, and he looked with respect at the rock.

"Hey, the tide's out and the sand's nice and hard, let's play Star Ball," yelled Tan Buck.

Everyone scurried to find themselves four nice round small stones while Tan Buck dug four holes in the sand at the four points of a star shape. Each hole was about two knuckles wide and three knuckles deep. One by one, the children stood at the centre and tried to roll their pebbles, one into each hole. Young Beaver got all four pebbles in so he got another turn but only sunk two the next try. After three tries each, Young Beaver still had the highest score so he was declared the winner.

Then they gathered up their clams and headed for home. The village was a hive of activity, preparing for potlatch!

Chapter Twelve

Potlatch

The people of the village ran down to the beach to see an impressive sight. The high carved prows of two forty-foot traveling canoes raced for the shore, side by side, their paddlers in perfect time with each other, loudly chanting their travelling song. Standing with one foot on the prow of each canoe, was Chief Eagle Feather of the great Qualicum village. As the canoes reached the shore, the paddlers back-paddled suddenly and their chief leapt to the shore, as agile as a deer, splendid in his intricately patterned blanket and wide-brimmed hat. Cheers of greeting rose up and men ran down to help lift the canoes onshore. Chief Eagle Feather was escorted up to the doorway of Chief Grey Fox's longhouse, where he was greeted with warmth and ceremony and welcomed inside.

All day long, more canoes arrived, bearing families of the Comox, Saanich, Cowichan,

Tsawassen, Musqueam and even the Squamish villages for the great Potlatch. No matter how many arrived, all were greeted warmly, and found a place to rest and offered food and drink. Some of their villages were only one hands-breadth of the sun's journey away by canoe, but others had traveled a day or two or even three to attend.

By day there were athletic contests for the men and boys; spear and harpoon throwing, shooting arrows through tossed rings, running and swimming. Golden Eye and Tan Buck were in charge of lining up the targets and keeping the starting lines clearly marked, but they joined in the competitions too. It was great fun and very exciting to visit with their cousins from Protector Island and to make new friends from other villages. Young children watched from their perches on top of the longhouse. The women shared news and played their favorite gambling games, betting with their caches of beaver teeth.

After sunset on each of the five days of this potlatch, everyone entered the great longhouse and was made comfortable and offered delicious food. Smoked and fresh cooked oysters, clams, salmon, halibut, cod, sea urchins, crab, seal, deer, duck and swan were served on long, animal-shaped platters. Each group of guests sang their own song of thanks for the food and to the cooks. Women carried around seal bladders full of rich, delicious oolachon oil and filled bowls with it, into which the people dipped their meat and fish.

Next, baskets of steamed camas, plus rush and lily roots, wild onions and parsnips were passed around followed by canoe-shaped bowls of fresh and dried blueberries, salmonberries, thimbleberries, and huckleberries. Many boiling bags of salal tea made the rounds plus bladders of icy cold spring water, served in intricately carved cups of maple and alder; the cups themselves to be given as gifts to the guests.

When all were satisfied, the platters and bowls were removed by the women and girls. Chief Grey Fox arose on his high platform and began the evening's ceremony. He welcomed his fellow chiefs, relatives and neighbours. He and other elders of his village told tales of their history and heritage. Official names and honours, marriages and dowries, rights and privileges were declared, including the official announcement that Golden Eye would become the next Great Chief.

Gifts were then presented to the guests. According to the rank of each guest, they were offered furs, woven blankets, storable foods, shields, hats, decorated garments or pouches of spiral dentalia shells, because the richness and the abundance of the gifts reflected the wealth and stature of the host village.

By the receiving of the gifts, the guests acknowledged that they were now aware of the changes to status, names and rights.

On the last night, as on each night of this potlatch, as the children settled on their mothers' and fathers' laps, the entertainment for the evening began. Planks were laid between two wooden blocks and pounded upon as the drumbeat began. Low chanting was heard coming from behind screens and outside the door. With a great flourish, the dancers and singers entered. The singers twirled rawhide and shell tambourines, and the dancers shook their rattles of deer hooves on sticks or beautifully carved, small pebble-filled boxes on handles. In their fantastic masks and capes they appeared as great beasts and birds and spirits both good and evil. Their dances portrayed myths and legends or marvelous acts of heroism of their own or of their ancestors. Whistles of wood and bullroarers - flat sticks whirled at the end of a rope - added sound effects along with the din of pounding on the walls and stomping on the roof of the longhouse. Great flashes of fire and smoke erupted as shamanic powders were thrown into the great central fire.

Golden Eye and Tan Buck were part of the sound effects team, pounding on the outer walls and roof, competing to see who could make the guests jump in fear the most, but something they saw was causing them fear of their own.

"Isn't that Screaming Jay?" whispered Tan Buck.

"Yes, it is," replied Golden Eye solemnly.

"It looks like he's going to do his spirit dance next. I'd recognize that orange raven's beak on his mask anywhere."

"But didn't he take off this morning after the throwing and shooting competition? He was so furious at that man, Ten Trees, for beating him at his specialty, the three ring shot. Just because he's the best shot here doesn't make him the best shot everywhere!"

"Yes, I thought he was going to strangle Ten Trees right there and then, but he just took off running. He runs for hours sometimes, I've seen him, all alone, just running and running. He's a strange one all right.

Hey, what's that he's putting into that bladder of tea?"

"We'd better keep an eye on him," intoned Tan Buck. "He's probably going to drink something to make him even wilder than usual. Maybe we should warn your father."

"We don't want to disturb the dances. Let's just watch him closely."

Screaming Jay and his entourage entered the longhouse with a grand flourish of rattles, drums, coloured smoke and his own long, high screech. People pulled their blankets tighter around their shoulders, and children hid behind their parents and peeked out. Round and round he danced, lunging and spinning, pretending to attack and then whirling away.

Then, in what seemed like a gesture of honour, of acknowledgement of the champion, he drew from beneath his black-feathered cape a cup of exceeding beauty, the bowl covered in mother of pearl with the base decorated in dentalia outlined with gold. He

offered it to Ten Trees then drew forth a small bladder of tea and filled the cup.

Ten Trees accepted the apparent grand gesture and brought the bowl to his lips as Screaming Jay whirled, ran and leapt, screeching, out the door and into the night. He appeared to have turned himself into a jaybird and flown away.

Golden Eye charged into the longhouse.

"Don't drink that, Ten Trees!" he shouted, but it was already too late.

Ten Trees rose, staggering, shrieking and tearing at his hair and clothing and trying to pull out his eyes and his tongue. On and on he raved and thrashed. No one could get near him to try to help. Finally, he fell screaming to the floor, writhing in agony.

Parents had hurried their little ones out of the longhouse so that their dreams would not be haunted by the horrible sight. The elders and the shamans gathered around Ten Trees, chanting and sprinkling magic powders upon him. They carried him to the sweat lodge and tried to give him healing drinks but to absolutely no avail. His groaning and screaming continued, his mouth frothed and his eyes rolled back into his head. Finally, mercifully, Ten Trees body dropped to the ground and his spirit departed.

"Father, I think I know what killed him," Golden Eye whispered. "I believe Screaming Jay put some dried stinkweed in that bladder of tea. Tan Buck and I saw him preparing something out there and Grandmother Robin Song told me that is how a man dies from it."

"That is very true," intoned old Brown Bear, shaman of the Saanich village, "although I have not seen such a death since I travelled to the north of Protector Island. Some people up there use stinkweed to kill their enemies. They do it in front of everyone to prove how ruthless they are. I find it inhuman and am surprised that one of the People of the Salmon would do such a thing."

"Let us all return to the longhouse," said Grey Fox. "We were preparing to banish Screaming Jay if he came back because he has lost all reason! He has attacked my son here - see the arrow mark in his arm? Only because Golden Eye is protected by strong spirits is he still alive. Let's go now and perform the banishment ceremony. Tomorrow runners will be sent to find him and inform him never to return to the villages of the Salish People. He will be welcome nowhere among good people. Let the spirits do with him what they will."

Chapter Thirteen

The Children's Potlatch

The potlatch guests had departed. Golden Eye looked around the village and saw all his young friends and cousins sitting around, morosely dwelling on the fearful events of the previous day. Something had to be done to cheer them up, he thought.

"Hey, you kids," he called. "Come and help me build up this fire. A nice fire is always so cheery."

No one moved.

"I'll tell you a story," Golden Eye cajoled.

One by one, smiles replaced frowns and the children got up and began dragging or carrying wood to the fire, animated by the promise of a good tale. One by one they gathered around the leaping, crackling fire and looked intently at Golden Eye, who remained standing with his face to the watery, autumn sun.

"Sit down, my friends, and I will tell you the story of how I caught fifty fish in one afternoon!"

With words, with gestures of his hands, with body motions and with facial expressions, Golden Eye wove a storyteller's tale.

"One summer day, with the sun shining golden on Arms Wide Bay, I set out to catch some salmon for smoking to help fill your fat, hungry bellies all the long, cold winter. I ran through the forest, over to that place where Otter and Goose islands are close together and the water races wild and white over the big rocks there. On the other side of the rapids is a green and shady pool. There I have seen our brothers, the salmon, gather before they brave the rapids to get to their home. As sure a morning comes each day, there were many salmon there, maybe two hundred, big ones too. Oh, my stomach rumbled and my mouth watered just looking at them, but how could I catch them?

I sat on a big rock and I thought and I thought. I need some help here, I thought, but I was a long way from home with no other people around. Hmmm, what could I do?

Then an idea came to me, so I went into the forest and whispered to my old friend, Grumbly, the brown bear. You remember that I rescued Grumbly when he was a cub and fell into that pit? Well, I've been watching him grow all my life, tossing him a salmon now and then and picking huckleberries side by side with him before he goes for his long sleeps, so he owed me a favour. This day he had eaten many blackberries and was taking a nap in his favorite clump of ferns. He seemed willing to help so I led him to the edge of the forest near the green and quiet pool.

Then I ran up the island to the tip and leaned down to the water. I called to my other friend, Black Fin, the young killer whale. He was in a good mood because the sun was shining on his glossy black back, so he agreed to help me too.

Now it was time to put my plan into action. Quietly as a feather on the breeze and slowly as the porcupine waddles, I anchored my sturdy fishnet above the rapids and then walked through the water. I opened my net around one side of the fish pool and prayed in my mind to the spirits of the salmon to please give themselves to us for food. Then I slapped the water really hard with my free hand and I yelled out "NOW " to my friends.

Black Fin began swimming into the opening between me and the far shore, thrashing and splashing and making his fiercest, scary, open-mouth face. Arrrrrrrrr! Well, that scared those salmon so bad that they either swam into my net or swam toward shore and there waited Grumbly! He flipped them up onto the shore and they flopped all around like this, floppity, floppity, flop. And so I caught me fifty salmon!"

Golden Eye lay on his side, flipping about and opening and closing his mouth like a salmon. The little children jumped up and ran over to him, right in the

spirit of the story, pretending to try to catch the slippery salmon that was Golden Eye. The older ones laughed and drummed on their log seats.

"Hey, I have an idea," said Tan Buck. "Why don't we put on our own potlatch, a fun one, just by us kids. We can paint our faces like masks and make capes out of ferns and cedar fronds and act out our favorite stories, like Golden Eye just did. I can show you some easy dance moves."

"Yeah, and we can invite our parents to be our guests," chimed in White Daisies. "We'll make them pretend gifts of things like - like a big dark green leaf with a pile of red berries on it, or bird eggshells and feathers on a nice piece of driftwood, or paint a face on a big clam or oyster shell or maybe bouquets of flowers. We girls can do that, right?"

The other girls nodded in eager agreement.

"Excellent, my friends!" said Golden Eye. "This is just the thing to clear all our minds of bad memories and let us get back to enjoying life. Let's go!"

For two days the entire young population of the village scurried around, meeting secretly for practices and progress reports. On the third evening, as the adults gathered for the evening meal, the Young People of the Salmon put on their show.

"Great and honoured friends, welcome to our humble potlatch," declared Golden Eye.

"What?" "What's going on?" came expressions of surprise from the grownups.

"Please, take your seats in our grand, open-air longhouse with the heavens for a roof. Receive the gifts with which we show our gratitude for your long journeys."

Quickly, the girls took over serving the meal, adding special treats like salmon roe and smoked clams to make it a grand feast. Parents and grandparents chuckled and got into the spirit of the evening, complimenting the chefs. They exclaimed over the humble but beautiful gifts that the little children carried to them, walking ever so carefully in order not to drop or spill them. Black Sparrow cried - her happiness always spilled over liquidly from her eyes.

Then as the meal was finished, Golden Eye arose again and clapped his hands sharply. Green Duck began beating on a small plank drum and his sisters, Spotted Trout and Red Fox began to chant. Out of the gathering dusk, from behind the trunks of grand old trees entered the dancers.

"Behold the Haida Legend of How The Raven Stole The Sun." proclaimed Golden Eye.

With branches for wings, Tan Buck portrayed that great trickster and bringer of the necessities of life, The Raven. Black Loon danced grandly as the Sky Chief, holding a box with a yellow sun symbol on its side. The girl, Little Fawn, moved gently, representing the daughter of the Sky Chief.

"Raven grew tired of living in darkness and of seeing The People at the mercy of the ghosts and spirits because they could not see," chanted Golden Eye.

Raven produced a cup of water, whirled about, passed it to Sky Chief's daughter and then leapt behind a big log.

"Raven had turned himself into a pine needle and fell into the cup."

Sky Chief's daughter raised the cup and drank, swallowing the needle. Immediately her belly began to swell (Little Fawn tucking a doll under her skirt). Soon, mimicking birth, she pulled the doll from under her skirt.

"Thus was Raven born as the precious grandson of the Sky Chief. He quickly grew," chanted Golden Eye.

Young Beaver, a lad of six summers sat down on the doll and rocked and rubbed his eyes, mouth open, as if he was crying.

"Clever, clever Raven," chanted Golden Eye. "He pretended to be irritable, knowing that his grandfather would do anything to please him."

Black Loon as Sky Chief bent and nodded over Raven, turning his head this way and that. How could he stop the child's screaming? Sky Chief brought the boy the wonderful box. Raven opened it and pulled out the sun (a bouquet of yellow flowers)!

Young Beaver scuttled away and Tan Buck jumped into his place.

"Raven grabbed the Sun and escaped into the sky!" loudly chanted Golden Eye as Tan Buck leapt to the top of a large driftwood root where he smeared his face with soot that had been cached there.

"Thus Raven changed from white to black from the soot of the smoke-hole and thus he put the sun in the sky to give light and warmth to The People!"

Even before the praise for this dance stopped, six of the older children entered the circle and stood about, holding aloft branches. They represented a forest. Then four small children, carrying berry baskets began to creep in. Toe-heel, toe-heel, they danced, in time with the drumming and chanting.

The tone of the drum slowed to a sombre pitch, as did the chanting. White Daisies, hunched over, wearing an old brown blanket, with long strands of dried grass for a grey wig, represented an old grandmother and stood at the edge of the "forest".

"Beware, children of the Kwakiutl," she cried. "Beware Dzunuk'wa, the Wild Woman of the Forest Who Eats Children!" Then she turned and went away.

The berry pickers danced about the trees, pretending to fill their baskets, peering around from time to time, watching out for Dzunuk'wa. Suddenly, the branches of the "trees" began to swish and sway. The drumbeats became louder and faster, the chanting louder and higher as a tall figure, cloaked in a cape of

squirrel tails, with stringy roots for hands and bull kelp for hair slithered into their midst. It was Dzunuk'wa, black-faced and sleepy-eyed and she uttered her strange cry "U, hu, u, u."

With sinuous motions, Dzunuk'wa (Brown Wren) beckoned hypnotically to the children, offering them bright things and pretty things. The children fell under her spell and began to follow her. At the far edge of the forest, Dzunuk'wa opened her arms wide and the children began to gather under her cape. She enclosed them, giving the effect of having put them in her basket. Then she fell asleep.

Into the forest rushed Golden Eye, wearing a shaman's bear headdress. He searched and searched for the lost children and finally spied Dzunuk'wa asleep with the children still writhing about in her basket. Golden Eye appeared to change himself into angry old black bear, Crooked Paw, by flipping a bearskin about his shoulders. He crept silently over to the sleeping Dzunuk'wa and with one great swipe of his claws (a forked piece of tree root), ripped open her basket. Out jumped the children, whole and healthy!

They danced their thanks to Old Crooked Paw, who doffed his costume and turned back into Great Shaman Golden Eye. The children ran away home, never to wander too far into the forest again!

As the cheers for this dance died down, into the circle hopped Tan Buck as Raven and Green Duck, costumed with clusters of dried grass, as Pheasant in a Salish legend. Raven had a fishing rod, and as he danced he seemed to haul in many fish. Pheasant danced around Raven, and seeing the great pile of fish, begged Raven for some of them. Raven refused. Pheasant danced his disappointment, but then straightened up and indicated that he would go and shoot himself a deer. Raven laughed but followed the pheasant. From out of the forest ran a deer (the girl, Young Birch, in a deer-hide robe holding forked-branch antlers to her head), chased by the Great Spirit in the form of a man (Squirrel Tail).

Green Duck as Pheasant mimicked shooting the deer dead.

"The pheasant shoots straight," indicated the man. Pheasant showed no pride. Then the man indicated, "You will not be able to carry that deer all the way home."

Sure enough, the pheasant's wife (Spotted Fawn) had to help him carry it the last few yards to his home.

Then Raven sent his sons with some salmon to trade for some deer meat. Pheasant refused to trade and this angered Raven. Soon the children of the Raven and the children of the Pheasant (small children dusted with charcoal or ash) had a war, the raven children throwing fish and the pheasant children throwing grease. Raven sat in the middle and caught and ate the deer grease. Then the children went home.

Up jumped Raven, and he shot a deer that was chased by a man.

The man indicated, "Raven can shoot straight." Raven puffed himself up, shaking his bow.

"I shoot straight because I am Raven, the very best of all creatures."

"This deer will be too heavy for you to carry all the way home," indicated the man.

Raven scoffed and dragged the deer away but indeed, it did become too heavy. Raven danced off to his house and dancing, gestured to his wife to go and get the deer. However, when she arrived, the deer had turned into a hollow log (Young Birch threw away her antlers and stretched out straight).

"And thus Raven was repaid for his pride with an empty belly," chanted the man and the dance was done.

All the young dancers, drummers, and chanters entered the great circle and raised their right arms, cheering for themselves along with their parents and grandparents.

They were rewarded with blueberries in honey and huckleberry juice and beamed with pleasure from the praise and thanks they were given. The whole village slept much more happily that night.

Chapter Fourteen

Countdown to Vision Quest

Golden Eye had made his long run for the day. He had run all the way to the northern tip of the island, to sit amidst the fourteen salty springs. Water burbled up, leaving an odd, whitish rim surrounding them. No trees grew in their midst, nor any ferns or bracken, only brown, bent grass and pink-flowered sea blush.

Golden Eye liked to be there. It was a place like none other on this island or any other place he had visited. Its strangeness and singularity seemed to help him clear his mind.

Today, for the first time he felt the nearness of something, something he couldn't touch or see, something that seemed to pulsate, almost like a drumbeat, something that seemed to be trying to speak inside his head.

He looked away to the place he had chosen for his vision quest - a high bluff, shaped like a hook, on the east side of his island, and facing across the other islands toward the Big Land. Old One Eye, the black wolf walked silently, into the circle, wary of the bubbling water. He lay down next to Golden Eye, head on his forelegs.

"What do you think, old friend?" Golden Eye asked the wolf, who raised his head questioningly. "Do you think I'm ready? Does anyone ever know if they are ready to step out, to go away from family and home? I wonder if this will change me; and what if my spirit is stolen while I am in a trance? Only one way to find out I guess, just go and do it."

One golden eye peered into another. The wolf tipped his head to the side, trying to understand.

"Come on, old friend," Golden Eye called. "Run

home with me and see if you can keep up this time," he joked, although Old One Eye was now well past his prime.

Golden Eye dipped his hand into one of the springs and let the salty water run down his back; a ritual he had created for himself. It felt somehow like he was connected with the earth and the sea at once, connecting his sweat with that of the earth; then off he ran.

Boy and wolf loped through the forest and meadows, past the two northern mountains, and across stony beaches. They leapt across the chasm created by the waterfall high above Many Clams Beach. They both stopped to drink from a cold, tumbling creek halfway home. As they reached the clearing, Golden Eye knew the moment that Old One Eye had left his side. There was only one human with whom the wolf felt comfortable, connected and safe - Golden Eye.

Everyone was busy at the longhouse, laying in stores for the winter and preparing for a village feast that night in honour of Golden Eye's vision quest.

A new ten-man trade canoe was taking shape on the beach above tide line, and a number of young men were unloading a canoe full of oysters. Hot, low, old fires were sending up ripples of heat. People were spreading filleted salmon on racks above the fires and space was made for the oysters as well, as they were shucked by a veritable team.

Golden Eye got out his own short, sturdy, stone knife and pitched in. Tan Buck and his father, Whispering Grass, had dug a pit and built a long fire in it and placed stones among the logs of firewood. Now that the fire had burned down and the stones were very hot, layers of seaweed were placed over the stones and then baskets of fresh clams and oysters spread over top. More seaweed was added and the whole works was covered with beach rocks and sand. A tube of bull kelp extended from the top to the hot stone level in order to add water to make lots of steam.

Those women not filleting salmon were busy scraping deer and bear hides from yesterday's hunt or spinning dog and goat fur for weaving or making cakes of cranberries and salal berries. The old ones dug camas root – a potato-like tuber – plus wild onions and parsnips.

Young children were busy too: boys having fast-climbing contests or kicking around their woven balls, girls playing family with their dolls.

The nights and mornings were becoming crisper although the days were still hot. There had been no rain for two weeks and dry leaves swished and crackled on the forest floor and blew out onto the beach.

As the sun began to set, the pit was uncovered and a feast of steamed clams and oysters, dipped in oolachon grease rewarded them for their labours. Little cakes made of pounded fern root and fish eggs were passed around too, along with boiled onions. Everyone had all they wanted to eat and contented talk and laughter was shared too.

"So, tomorrow's the big day for you Golden Eye," said grandfather Strong Oak. "You'll be on your way for your vision quest."

"I think we should have one last good sweat lodge before you go," said Grey Fox, "to sweat the smell of humans out of you so you'll be more acceptable to the spirits."

"And not such an invitation to cougars and other hungry beasts either," added Tan Buck giving away his worry about his friend's long time alone.

"Sounds good to me," smiled Golden Eye.

"We'll get the fire going. You go check on what you're taking with you then come and join us in a little while," said the shaman, Strong Oak.

"I'll help you with that," offered Whispering Dawn.

So, Golden Eye and his gentle mother checked his few supplies and packed the new cape and loincloth she had lovingly made for him.

Then he went to be alone for a few minutes.

Chapter Fifteen

Connections

Golden Eye sat on the big square granite rock at the end of the beach overlooking the ocean and leaned against the trunk of a red cedar. He turned his face up to the full moon glowing above and prayed.

"Great Spirit, you are so near me. I feel you pass into my body and mind as I sit here on this great rock by the sea. This great red cedar at my back is so strong. I give thanks that you saw fit to put so many of them here for us. They and the salmon are our great treasure.

Tonight the moon is full and I can see its talking face. Why am I drawn to sit in its silver glow? I see its light dance on the little waves, white like eagle down, and I wonder if the fish under the water also gaze up at it. The moon looks like a mother, singing me a lullaby. I feel so peaceful under her.

The few clouds above me are dark as the sky and yet a little different from it. They were white during the

day and then pink and purple at sunset, but now they have turned bluish-black. When they pass by the moon I can almost feel myself inside them, floating along, all misty and sparkling in its light.

I have much to ponder. Strong Oak, our shaman, has told me that perhaps I am the returned spirit of a lone wolf that used to live near our village. He never attacked or stole our food, just slipped through the forest, pausing to watch the doings of the village, like my friend Old One Eye. Strong Oak says I have studied enough with him and the elders and learned all he can teach me of the spirit world.

Tomorrow I go on my vision quest to determine my true vocation and find my own spirit guide. I think I am ready. I can feed and shelter and protect myself. It's the spirit search that puzzles me. What will happen when I sit alone by the fire and throw the special powder into the fire and meditate?

I know I must open myself to welcome my spirit guide, but I cannot help but feel a little fear. I want to still be myself when I come back, but I need to find the direction, the path I must follow, as I become a man.

My need to learn is stronger than my fear I think, and that's good.

Thank you for this pleasant breeze, Great Spirit. I believe you have sent it to tell me to go and join the men in the sweat lodge, so I will heed you. Thank you for this beautiful world and my time upon it. Please keep safe the families of my village while I am away."

The men were already inside the sweat lodge as Golden Eye entered. Raven Tail threw more water on the hot rocks and a great cloud of steam arose, cedar-scented from the branches laid upon the rocks. They talked of the day's catch and the signs of an early winter.

"So, tell us what you have learned from this old grey-head, Strong Oak," queried Black Cod. "Has he prepared you well for your quest?"

"Yes. The most important lesson to learn was to listen, all the time, with all my senses, to listen. He explained about the many-layered spirit world that fits over the earth like an upside down bowl. He told me how, in the beginning all was in darkness and humans, animals and ghosts dwelt together. All were similar but humans had little power. The animals of the land and sea had more because they could transform into humans, beasts or fish at will. The ghosts were the most powerful though, because they were invisible and constantly sought to devour souls as well as food.

He taught me that Raven brought the sun and

moon and fire to the people, which banished the ghosts to the darkness and gave people more power and wisdom so that they could begin to live in harmony with the plants and animals. He warned me of Thunderbird, bringer of death, whose nest is on the dead volcano, how he kills the whales that he eats by throwing down lightning bolts when he blinks and how he makes thunder by the beating of his great wings.

He also warned me of tricksters and transformers - spirits who can lead people into danger and death. He told me too of the home of the salmon people far beneath the sea from which they come every year to offer themselves to us for food. Therefore we must return every bone of our first salmon to the ocean to honour them and thank them so that they will return each year.

Most importantly though, I learned that there is a spirit in every single thing. I learned that we must listen to them and be in harmony with them; always asking permission and offering a small gift to their spirit if we must kill them to eat or use them to make our homes, our clothes, our tools and our medicine.

Where I go now, I must allow my spirit to journey to the spirit world, to seek that one which will guide and protect me throughout my life. I sincerely hope I am ready."

There was a long pause as the men thought about what Golden Eye had said, wondering if they should add any words of wisdom or caution and deciding they should not.

"Well, it sounds like you are ready. You're certainly getting tall and strong," mused Grey Fox as he threw a little more water on the rocks. "We'll try to struggle along here without you," he said with a smile. "We might still be here or we may have moved back to the winter village; it all depends on the weather."

Golden Eye yawned and looked around the circle in the sweat lodge at his father, his cousins, his uncles and his grandfather. He thanked the Great Spirit for such a good family, then he and they went off to bed, his last night at home before his vision quest!

Chapter Sixteen

White Water

"Tan Buck, wake up," whispered Golden Eye.

"What? What's wrong? What do you want?" muttered the sleepy lad.

"Shhh. I want one last canoe ride with my best friend before I leave. Let's go."

"Is it light out yet?"

"Just about. Come on sleepyhead; or should I take Fat Goose instead?"

"I'm up, I'm up," he yawned. "Lead on fearless leader."

Dew lay heavy on the moss and trees and a single raven croaked in the still-dark branches. Silently the boys carried Golden Eye's canoe down the beach and leapt into it even as it slid away from shore - a bird freed from its cage - a magic carpet waiting for its orders.

"Where to?" whispered Tan Buck.

"The rapids!"

"Yes! The rapids! The perfect last ride! Can't you paddle any faster?"

"Me? Get up off your fat behind and show me what you're made of!"

Off through the morning mist the two friends paddled out of Arms Wide Bay, wheeling westward, on their way to Sansum Narrows. The tide was about to turn and the water in the narrows would indeed be white. Behind them the first rays of the sun pierced the sky above Tan Buck's favorite snow-wrapped mountain on the Great Land, splashing gold on the wavelets before the canoe.

"The tide's running the other way. We'd better portage over Burial Island if we want the best ride," declared Golden Eye.

"Right, let's pull in here where it's nice and sandy."

"This will give me a chance to pay my respects to my ancestors before I leave too," said Golden Eye breathlessly as they lifted the canoe out of the water and carried it, one on each side.

"Okay, but let's not hang around too long. We want to catch the full tide rush through the narrows. Brrr. I just remembered that story about Shuh Shu Cum and all the hair stood up on the back of my neck. I'll be watching for his corpse going through there - or his ghost."

"There are enough ghosts on this island to suit me. Look at some of those old coffins up in the trees there - they're so old there's moss all over them - and old dead branches. It looks like arms sticking out of the coffins."

"Shut up! I'm scared enough already - let's go!" yelped Tan Buck.

"Here, up in this tree is where my father's grandfather's bones are resting. Hey, look over there!"

Golden Eye stopped short and Tan Buck stumbled. They set the canoe down.

"What is it?" asked Tan Buck, panting, grateful for the rest.

"Someone's been staying here. Look, you can see where the ferns and moss are all bent and squashed."

"And there's what's left of a small campfire! You're right, but who would want to stay in such a creepy place? They'd have to be crazy!"

"I only know one crazy person, don't you?"

"Screaming Jay!" they whispered together.

"Let's get out of here before he comes back," whispered Golden Eye.

"I'm right behind you. I'm just worried about who's right behind me!"

As the boys reached for the canoe, they heard a cracking noise above them. Golden Eye shoved Tan Buck to the left and leapt to the right himself as a big dead branch crashed onto the ground where they had stood. Wide-eyed, the boys hoisted the canoe and made tracks for the narrows. Once they had the canoe back in the water, with now bright sunlight blazing all around, they put their fears to rest.

Ahead lay Sansum Narrows; it's tide-rip roaring, white foam leaping skyward as it crashed into the boulders that clustered in the watery pass.

"Yahoo, let's do it!" yelled Tan Buck over the roar of the water.

"Keep it straight down the centre of the channel. We have to keep away from the whirlpool," yelled back Golden Eye. "Shuh Shu Cum or not, we don't want to get sucked down into it."

Leaning forward, paddling with all their might, the boys launched themselves into the narrows. Golden Eye in front steered the prow, deftly switching his paddle from the left to the right, the feel of his canoe beneath him telling him which way to go. Tan Buck in the stern used his paddle unerringly as a rudder in the boiling stretches and then swiftly changed to paddling when they gained some headway.

The water churned and boiled, roaring like a bottled hurricane, sometimes sliding green over the massive granite boulders, then frothing white again in the back eddies. Slipping, sliding through chutes of rushing white water, the boys bent their backs into the contest, knees pressed into the canoe bottom, toes

forced down for balance. As they came out of the big chute, a huge, swirling, slurping whirlpool appeared off their left stern and the stern of the canoe slid toward it.

"Dig, dig, dig!" yelled Golden Eye over the sound of the water. "Back paddle right!"

"It's nearly got us!" screamed Tan Buck.

"No! We're the two - strongest - bravest - young Salish - alive," panted Golden Eye. "Let's finish this."

The boys reached inside themselves for one last great burst of power and finally pulled away from the whirlpool. From there, the channel widened somewhat, so the two friends rested, just steering as they sped to the end of the island.

"Now that was fun!" crowed Tan Buck, "a close

call, but FUN!"

"Aren't you glad I got your lazy bones out of bed now?" chuckled Golden Eye.

From there it was an easy paddle to home. They arrived just in time for breakfast, after a swim and rinse and getting into dry clothes.

As soon as the meal was over, Golden Eye said his goodbyes and walked off, finally on his way to his vision quest.

Chapter Seventeen

Vision Quest at Last

North. North and then East he went. Golden Eye walked all the way, savouring every moment and every sensation of forest and field, meadow and beach. A mother skunk and her young family toddled across his path, following a rabbit trail. Golden Eye paused and smiled.

Three days postponed, three days after the fire, Golden Eye actually left; on his own. The fire had spared the longhouse, and most of the food supplies had been saved so the village could spare him now.

He used his spear as a walking stick to help him rise over fallen logs and moss-slippery rocks and to pole-jump over creeks and streams. Around his neck hung small pouches containing his few small necessities: his flint fire striker, a few herbs, a water bag, some of Strong Oak's trance-inducing powder and some strips of deer meat dried to chewable leather.

Alone, early fall breezes swirling his long, black hair about his face, Golden Eye became truly aware for the first time in his life that he was a person apart from all other persons, seeking his own truths, knowing the earth for himself. Alone.

Down the long valley path he walked, heading northward. Then he veered eastward down the long slope to the meadow where the giant old oak tree spread its long branches and to the sandy beach beyond. Along the scarred driftwood logs he wandered, wondering where they came from. What storm or landslide had ripped their big, strong roots from the earth and set them a-sail in the sea, to end up here on his island, a pale, wooden necklace for the spirits of the shore?

So focused was he on his journey's end that he didn't notice a following presence, or rather two following presences. His wolf companion was there of course, off to his left among the trees, but also, far back on his right flank, a much more menacing one – Screaming Jay!

Since his banishment he had hidden himself away in the deep forest, first on the burial island, then back on the Island of Salty Springs, making no permanent camp, building no fires which might give him away. He waited. He knew Golden Eye would be passing this way en route to his vision quest, and he waited for his last chance to destroy him. Hatred boiled in his gut for the boy who had survived all his attempts to kill him, to make the way clear for Green Duck to become Great Chief. He knew the boy was protected by strong spirits; but soon, while he was in his vision quest trance and unaware of his surroundings, Screaming Jay would make his move. He carried his lance lightly; awaiting his moment.

Where the beach ended at a jumbled pile of granite boulders, Golden Eye began his ascent. Yellowed grasses and tough, scrubby bushes survived on the exposed hillside. On top of the promontory, arbutus and pines spread their roots into whatever soil they could find. Golden Eye walked the length of the ridge top, all the way to the little bay nearly encircled by the claw-like hook of land. So calm was the little bay where, in years gone by, fishing parties had taken shelter from sudden storms in the straits or from raiders from the north!

Golden Eye turned and walked back to his chosen place. It was a broad, flat area of exposed granite surrounded on three sides by pine trees. On the fourth side stood the Five Sisters, an old, five-stalked arbutus tree; one stem arching in each of the four wind directions, the fifth bent and twisted over the edge of the cliff, as if staring down at the jagged, wave-splashed rocks below.

Golden Eye built his fire as the sun set, and then he gazed out across the water. One long swim across from him was Long Bone Island, with its giant, mushroom-shaped rock on the shore. Far beyond that, the Great Land faded into the purple mist of night.

The first night he just slept.

The next day he sat cross-legged before the fire, clearing his mind. He fasted. That night he built up the fire and cast into it some of Strong Oak's powder. Strange shapes appeared in the flames: weird dancers, masked faces, the face of the "lady in the water". Golden Eye no longer felt the hard rock beneath him. His face seemed to melt into the fire scenes. He felt light. He thought he heard faint singing, chanting, coming from within the fire. Finally he slept.

The third day, he sipped a little rainwater, ate just one bite of food then resumed his meditation. As the full moon rose, Golden Eye cast more magic powder into the flames. He brushed a little of Strong Oak's trance powder on the top of his fist and licked it cautiously.

The fire rose higher, smoke swirling around it, and wondrous colours appeared. Golden Eye became very aware of the figures within the smoke and the flames. He heard the songs of the dancers in the fire, voices issuing from fantastic masks.

"Welcome, searcher," the swirling, distorted voices whispered. "The spirits invite you to join them."

"Know that we have waited for you since you

left us to be born of woman."

"Many things will be required of you in this life. Many trails you must follow."

"Many people you will contact. You will share with them and they with you and one day, you will be the only one, the only leader left."

The face of the mysterious lady appeared.

"We will meet soon. I have secrets to share with you. Beware, beware!"

Louder and louder the voices grew. Larger and larger images appeared: great chiefs in full headdresses, a transparent shark's head - mouth open, the father of all salmon, and raven laughing.

Without warning a huge ghost-wolf seemed to leap at Golden Eye from his left side! So real was the vision that Golden Eye grasped the spear at his side and raised the tip while he leaned to the right.

A great, horrible scream woke Golden Eye from his trance. Something heavy passed over him. It was Screaming Jay, impaled on Golden Eye's spear and he continued his arc through the fire and out over the cliff he sailed!

Golden Eye rushed over to the edge. Far below, Screaming Jay's broken body glistened in the moonlight, eyes open, mouth twisted, gutting knife still clenched in his hand as the current slowly carried him away.

Golden Eye moved away from the grisly vision. Beyond the circle of firelight he saw a familiar sight; gleaming in the fire's glow, one golden eye looking into his own. And then they slept; the wolf and the boy with the wolf spirit, side by side by the crackling, lowering fire as the moon gazed down, and the crickets called. High above on a cedar limb a raven croaked a single note.

Chapter Eighteen

Hello, Goodbye, Hello

Golden Eye awoke the next morning to a golden, sunny day. West Wind swirled in the pine boughs and robins sang their let's-go-get-worms song. Golden Eye stretched his limbs that were stiff and aching from days of sitting and nights of sleeping on his granite precipice. He yawned and sat up. He reached for his water bag and drank a long, cool draught. Thirst quenched, he rummaged in his carrying pouch for some dried deer meat on which he munched hungrily, necessitating more water drinking.

His fire had one tiny red coal left, a miniature eye winking at him. Old One Eye was not in sight - off doing wolf things probably - but Golden Eye felt his nearness.

Golden Eye rose and stretched some more, bending his knees and his back and swinging his arms around. Then he remembered. The sound of waves lapping ashore drew him to the cliff edge and he looked down. Nothing. He saw nothing but the small waves throwing themselves upon the jumbled rocks and then being sucked back into the eternal ocean.

"Goodbye, Uncle," he called out, the wind carrying his words out over the water. "May your spirit find peace now."

"Well, I guess I'd better gather up my things and get going home," he muttered to himself. He stood still for a moment, searching his inner being. "I feel different. I really do. I feel connected to the entire world and to the spirit world as well, but I feel different too, like I'm a new person. I feel my pulse beating and I feel a rhythm around me, a quiet song, the song of the earth and the universe. And I have to stop talking to myself – One Eye, where are you?"

A cold nose touched the back of his right knee and Golden Eye yelped, jumped and spun around.

"Well, you can still surprise me, can't you boy? Come on, let's head home."

Off they went, the rising sun warming their left sides, ferns brushing against their legs, cobwebs and slug trails silvery before them, green frogs hopping off into the darker, wetter greenness. Homeward bound. The way seemed shorter, the air lighter in their lungs, and finally they climbed the last hill and looked down upon the roof of the longhouse where they saw the smoke of the communal fire rising straight up then tailing off to the East. Golden Eye set his feet on the last path toward home. Old One Eye went halfway with him and then, with a soft woof, melted away into the forest, his duty done.

Fat Goose was the first to see him coming and he let out a piercing shout.

"He's back. Golden Eye's back!" He ran toward his brother, his idol.

Golden Eye swooped him up and carried the squirming bundle into the compound. Circle upon circle of relatives formed around Golden Eye. Closest to him was a noisy, bouncing pack of children, all cheering and asking questions, one on top of the other. In the next orbit were the old ones who had been working near the fire and finally the young women and men, including Golden Eye's parents who were carrying little Silent Dawn. She stretched out her arms to Golden Eye and he reached for her and held her close while she ran her tiny hands through his long black hair and stroked his face. It was very good to be home. White Daisies smiled widely, but Tan Buck was nowhere to be seen.

Finally, when everyone was satisfied that he was whole and back safely in their fold they wandered off, back to their particular industry. Golden Eye went to sit in council with the elders for the first time. Their eyes were riveted on his face as he related the events of the last three days, culminating in the sad duty of informing them of his uncle's death. A silence fell upon the group.

"I think," said Strong Oak, the shaman, "that I speak for all of us in giving thanks to the Great Spirit for your successful vision quest and safe return home. I, too, hope that Screaming Jay's spirit finds rest and peace, but there is another reason we are glad that you are back."

Strong Oak looked around the circle into each face before continuing. Then he returned his gaze to Golden Eye.

"Last night your friend, Tan Buck, performed his final ritual for acceptance into the Dance Society. The ceremony was lead by Keen Arrow, Spirit Dance leader from the Saanich village, since Screaming Jay was no longer with us. All went well until Tan Buck had to release his spirit to the dance spirits for testing."

The old man lowered his gaze, took in a ragged breath and continued.

"Tan Buck's spirit did not return. His body lies in his family's place. He breathes but his eyes are empty. I was praying that you would return with enough spirit power to assist us in trying to bring Tan Buck's soul back into his body before it is too late."

"Of course we must do this," exclaimed Golden Eye. "Can we start right away?"

Golden Eye leaped to his feet, eager to begin the rescue.

"It is nearing dark," replied Strong Oak. "Old Brown Bear will arrive soon from Protector Island to add his power to ours. We must bathe to cleanse ourselves and gather in the sweat lodge while a large fire is built – one large enough to be seen in the spirit world. Then we will begin our search, sending out our spirits in a chain to find Tan Buck's and draw him back."

Within an hour, Strong Oak, Brown Bear and Golden Eye sat in a triangle around the massive, crackling fire. Tan Buck's inert body lay upon a bed of cedar boughs outside the triangle, his parents sitting, one on either side, silently holding his hands. The rest of the villagers stayed well back. The youngest children had already been put to bed to ensure that they did not disturb the intense focus of the searchers.

Strong Oak began the chant, entreating the occupants of the spirit world to hear them. Old Brown Bear took up the chant, asking that the spirits of the three be welcomed into the dark land. Golden Eye closed his eyes and he too began to chant. He called to Tan Buck's spirit, willing him to come near, to reach out to them.

From time to time Brown Bear and Strong Oak threw some of their magical powders into the fire, causing it to flare with bright colours and give off large clouds of glowing smoke.

After a time, Golden Eye felt as if he were

melting. He realized his spirit was leaving his body. He opened his eyes and observed the world of the spirits without losing his focus on finding Tan Buck's lost spirit. All about him was blackness - but a glowing blackness - and the presence of the spirits was very strong. Essences, vapours - strings of smoke they seemed to be - as they swirled or sped past Golden Eye's spirit. He thought he could hear the spirits but their sounds were felt more than heard.

Golden Eye strengthened his focus and contacted the spirits of Strong Oak and Brown Bear. As their spirits connected, their power more than tripled and Golden Eye was aware that he, or rather his spirit, shone.

With this combined strength they searched and called to Tan Buck. Suddenly, he was there with them, although he was indistinct, very vaporous.

Golden Eye reached for Tan Buck with his spirit. He called to him with memories of their strong friendship. Tan Buck's spirit seemed to respond, seemed to gather, then slipped away again, far out into the spirit world. Golden Eye felt the strong connection with Old Brown Bear, and he in turn was anchored in Strong Oak. Therefore, Golden Eye felt he could launch his spirit toward Tan Buck and away he soared, arrow-like.

Golden Eye came to Tan Buck's spirit and wrapped his spirit around that of his friend. Tan Buck's spirit became aware of his safety, aware of the love of his friend. Tan Buck brightened, filled with joy, and his spirit re-entered his body. Strong Oak reeled in the spirits of Brown Bear and Golden Eye, and they too returned to their bodies, exhausted and drained but extremely happy. Golden Eye jumped up and hugged Tan Buck.

The two friends whooped and hollered.

"You're back!"

"And you're back!"

"We're back!"

They jumped up and down, pounded each other on their backs, ran around the fire and then dove into the wonderful, salty ocean, still hollering their joy. Then they came back to the fire and hugged everyone they could get their hands on, especially Strong Oak and Brown Bear. People brought blankets to wrap them in and food and drink which the happy, happy boys gulped down with much gusto.

They were home, they were safe and they were together. Life was good and they could look forward to many years of friendship and adventures. The Coast Salish, the People of the Salmon, smiled and began to settle back into their timeless routine.

The End

Glossary

abundance	plenty
adze	arch-bladed tool for shaping wood
aura	a mist or glow surrounding one
caches	stores or supplies in one or more places
contorted	twisted in an unnatural manner
crenellated	notched, or with many dips and/or inlets
den	a home, lair or resting place of an animal
din	racket or noise
distended	swollen
domain	home or area under one's control
fasting	going without food for a period of time
garment	article of clothing
gunwale	top edge of a canoe's sides
harbour	a protected, deep-water body of water
hide	skin of an animal
infusion	a steeped brew or concoction
longhouse	permanent shelter for many families
nephrite	easily fractured hard stone of the jade family, giving sharp edges
obsidian	dark glass formed by hardened molten lava
potlatch	feast with gift-giving to announce changes in a particular group
poultice	medicated mass in cloth applied to sore area of the body
shaman	wise man and/or spiritual leader
spectre	ghostly vision
talking stick	stick to be held by one wishing to speak at a council meeting
thong	thin strip of leather for tying or lacing
zenith	the absolute top of something

Bibliography

Indian Tribes of B.C.
Reg Ashwell/Hancock House Publishers

Indians of the Northwest Coast
M. Bruggman, P. Gerber/Facts on File Publications

The Indians of Puget Sound: The Notebooks of Myron Eells
University of Washington Press

Cultures of the North Pacific Coast
H.B. Hawthorn,UBC/Harper and Row

Indian Herbalogy of North America
Alma R. Hutchens/Merco

Indian Art and Culture of the North West
Della Kew & P.E. Goddard/Hancock House Publishers

Sea and Cedar
Lois McConkey/T.J. McConkey Publ.

Handbook of American Indian Games
Allan MacFarlan, /New York, Dover

Native Peoples and Cultures of Canada, Chapter 8
Alan D. McMillan/Douglas & McIntyre

The First Nations of B.C.: An Anthropological Survey
Robert J. Muckle / UBC Press

The Gulf Islands Explorer - The Complete Guide
Bruce Obee / Gray's Publishing

Cedar
Hilary Stewart/Douglas & McIntyre

Native American Myths and Legends
Ed. Consult. Colin F. Taylor, PhD/Smithmark Publishers

When the Rains Came and other Legends of the Salish People
Dolly Bevan Turner/Orca Book Publishers

People of The Salmon
Canadian Museum of Civilization Corp./Civilization.ca

About the Author

Tell me a story! First it was me, begging my sister to read to me at bedtime – then it was my four little brothers, begging me to read to them. My head was filled with the adventures of children and magical beings, so it was only natural that I began to create my own stories. I fell in love with Salt Spring Island and all the rest of the super-natural coast of B.C. while boating with my own family and this, together with my fascination with legends, my childrens' Cherokee heritage, and my respect for the First Nations' way of life, gave rise to the Adventures of Golden Eye.

For the last fifteen years I have been immersed in theatre and as well, I have served in doctors' offices for thirty years while raising three sons and a daughter. Recently, I studied with the Institute of Children's Literature who gave me the final courage to put my stories out there.

And this is only the beginning. Golden Eye will go on to meet many other groups of First Nations people and learn of their ways and their legends and, of course, have lots more adventures!

ISBN 1425176828